Angel Lucifer

---◆---

Evil's Origin

---◆---

- A Novel -

Charles Simpson

Ascribe Publishing

P.O. Box 5726, L.I.C., NY 11105

http://homestead.juno.com/ascribepublishing

ISBN # 0-9700048-1-8

Angel Lucifer - Evil's Origin
An Introductory Poem

Coming over the horizon, I clearly could see
Things that were painful and much bigger than me.

I cried out to Jesus, with all of my soul
Not for deliverance, but simply to know:

No matter what comes, no matter what goes
My God is loving, and He's in control.

The answer did come, in such an amazing way
That it's hard to explain, even up to this day.

I caught such a glimpse, of the BRIGHTNESS of Him
Whose face always shines, and never grows dim.

Such holiness! Such majesty! Such utter, utter light;
Whatever is wrong, whatever's not right...

Simply can't be from Him. It must be from one
Who took what He gave, and made it undone.

Through the gift of free will, a light-bearer chose
To shut his own door, and evil arose.

Lovingly
dedicated
to the One
Whose amazing sacrifice at Calvary
delivered me from the powers of
darkness
A N D
redeemed
my lost
A N D
dying soul
f r o m
eternal damnation.

TABLE OF CONTENTS

INTRODUCTION

Many, including those who love the Lord and know that He is holy, have asked the questions:

* Since He is all-powerful, then why does God allow so much suffering, heartache, and horror to take place in the world in which we live?

* How can evil exist in a universe that a perfect God has created?

* If God is the Creator of all, does this mean He is also the Author of evil?

Hundreds of years before Christ people were struggling with these same thoughts. Epicurus (341-270 B.C.) wrote, "Either God wants to abolish evil, and cannot; or He can, but does not want to; or He cannot and does not want to. If He wants to, but cannot, He is impotent. If He can, but does not want to, He is wicked. But if God both can and wants to abolish evil, then how comes evil in this world?" How can we reconcile our Scriptural convictions that the God of the Bible possesses unlimited goodness, justice, and power, with the harsh reality that evil events are constantly occurring in the world around us?

Surely, these are penetrating questions, topics that the Bible is not reluctant to address. The Scriptures teach us that Adam's deliberate rebellion and disobedience caused all of mankind to be born into a fallen world. **(Romans 5:12-19)** Although the fall of man answers some theological questions, yet many remain. In the "perfect" Garden of Eden, even before Adam's fatal choice, we find a serpent speaking and spreading evil lies. **(Genesis 3:1-3)** The puzzle of evil is vastly incomplete without looking at the legacy of " . . . **that old serpent, the Devil.**" **(Revelation 20:2)** Even as we discover truths from God's Word, there will still be many unanswered questions this side of eternity. But without the Bible to guide and instruct us, the puzzle of evil would be absolutely and hopelessly unsolvable. The Bible does show us how sin came into existence. Speaking of Lucifer, it says, *"You were perfect in your ways from the day you were created, till iniquity was found in you." (Ezekiel 28:15)* Here is the origin of evil: unrighteousness found in a being who moments earlier was labeled as blameless. How in the world (or rather, how in the heavens!) could he make such a decision, and bring upon himself such a downfall? Once an anointed angel in heaven, Lucifer has somehow turned into the adversary of God's people and the enemy of all that is right and holy and good. Using the Biblical glimpses of his demise as our framework, I paint a parable about this diabolical transformation in which Lucifer, the Light-bearer, eventually became Satan, the slimy, seductive hater of God. By looking at his beginning, and using some imagination and inspiration, while remaining within the parameters of Biblical revelation, perhaps we can get a better understanding of the origin and essence of evil. (I use the word inspiration in the context of hoping that this story inspires you to trust God more and more. Only the Holy Scriptures are divinely inspired and infallible, that is, "God-breathed" and without error. So, for the sake of clarity, throughout this novel the Scriptures will be in bold print. Therefore, only what is bold can I say—with boldness—is without a doubt, the pure truth. Another word I'd like to add here. Knowing the power of the printed word, I personally would like to know where the author stood with the Lord before I'd read a book he wrote about Lucifer. I am a born-again, Bible-believing, Jesus-loving Christian!)

On occasion, a picture can truly be worth a thousand words. I believe the Biblical glimpses of Lucifer's transformation can bring more clarity to our perplexing universe than a thousand volumes of philosophy. With this hope, I try to elaborate on what is written by carefully adding color and details to a pencil sketch, without taking anything away or in any way disrespecting the original, divinely inspired drawings.

I begin with the Apostle Paul as he is ministering as recorded in the Book of Acts. As he is given insight into Lucifer's downfall, he comes to realize that God has created the best of all possible worlds. I then explore what others have said about this fascinating subject of the origin of evil and how these truths can best be incorporated into our lives today.

Humbly speaking about himself, the Apostle Paul told the early church in Corinth, *"I know a man in Christ who fourteen years ago—whether in the body I do not know, or whether out of the body I do not know, God*

11

knows—such a one was caught up to the third heaven. He was caught up into Paradise and heard inexpressible words, which it is not lawful for a man to utter." **(2 Corinthians 12:2-4)** Did this take place, as many Bible scholars believe, when they apparently stoned Paul to death outside the city of Lystra, as recorded in the Book of Acts? Possibly. And perhaps everything he learned while in Paradise wasn't unlawful for him to speak about. Perhaps the story unfolded like this . . .

ONE
A DAY TO REMEMBER

As Paul awoke early one morning, he noticed the sun was just beginning to peek its rays over the eastern horizon, commanding the darkness of night to flee just from the mere brightness of its rising. He slowly rolled the thick blankets off, sat up in bed and gazed around the one-room cottage. He and his traveling companion, Barnabas, had rented a small, quaint house on the edge of the town of Lystra in the region of Laconia in Asia Minor. As the darkness inevitably gave way to the light of morning, Paul noticed the fire in the hearth from the night before was still producing a small ribbon of continuous smoke. Off to one side of this room was a large, oak table completely cluttered with canvas material, small pieces of wood, and an assortment of tools. To help pay the expenses of their costly missionary journeys, Paul had became a tentmaker and Barnabas was a woodcarver by trade. Barnabas at one time had carved all types of unholy wooden idols and statues, but not anymore. Now, only wooden spoons and forks and other useful household items were fashioned by his skillful hands.

Paul quickly yet quietly dressed, hoping not to disturb his companion's sleep. Barnabas had a hard day previously and should sleep as long as he needed to, Paul reasoned. He put some items in his leather pouch, opened and quietly shut the door behind him, and headed out to the hills that surrounded the small city.

The morning air, crisp and invigorating, welcomed

him as he stepped outside. There were numerous wildflowers nearby, casting their many scents along the path that wrapped around the base of the hills the town was snuggled between. It was early spring and the dogwood trees were in full bloom, along with tulips and daffodils galore. The sun was now shining brightly in some areas, while dense fog still covered much of the low-lying valleys. After a while, Paul left the beaten path and headed straight up a large incline. He was walking briskly, hoping to get some needed exercise. His strength soon gave out, and he sluggishly and somewhat painfully made his way up to the top. "I'm not as young as I used to be," he humorously admitted to himself as he reached the summit. He leaned his right hand against a large maple tree, gasping for air as he soaked in the warm, morning sunshine. Paul was not a tall man, but his body was stout and solid; much like his soul.

He looked back in the direction from which he came, fondly remembering the days when he was able to run up such hills with the strength and exuberance of a young deer. As a boy growing up in Tarsus, skipping and hiking through the countryside was one of his favorite pastimes. He made his way to a large, fallen tree that afforded him a convenient bench to sit upon and rest his legs. As he looked out over the fog banks that covered the sleepy town below, his mind kept going back to happy childhood memories. He remembered well how he was both nervous and excited when he was privileged to move to Jerusalem as a teen. He was one of a chosen few, carefully selected from among thousands of applicants to attend school under the tutelage of the famous scholar Gamaliel. His favorite class back then was philosophy. He vividly remembered when most of the students, himself included, would debate into the early hours of the morning over different views of the world, of God, and of other mind-stretching ideals. One of their favorite debate topics was regarding the origin of sin and evil. Some of the students, though Jewish in background and nationality, espoused the various and popular ideas of Plato, Aristotle, and Socrates. These young, avid followers of Greek philosophy showed how powerfully Greek culture had cast its influence throughout the entire world since Alexander the Great's international conquests over three hundred years earlier.

Paul, however, had not allowed himself to be persuaded to embrace any school of thought that did not match up with his beloved Torah and the writings of the Old Testament prophets. The majority of the Jewish rabbis of his day, sad to say, embraced about as many different views as the mythological and philosophical Greeks on these types of subjects. So many of these blind religious leaders would allow fanciful myths and silly fables to influence their thinking to the point that they became even more confused than the heathen. This had revolted Paul as a young man, and in his heart he vowed to stay vehemently faithful to the sacred Scriptures, no matter what the cost. To fulfill this solemn vow to Jehovah God, Paul knew it meant he would have to study, learn, memorize, and understand as much of the Torah and the Prophets as he possibly could. His life's passion became to know God's Word, inside and out. More than one teacher remarked that Saul of Tarsus (as he was thus named before his dramatic Damascus Road conversion) knew the Holy Scriptures perhaps better than anyone else his age.

As he sat on the old, dead tree, he pulled out from his pouch a scroll of the book of Isaiah, affectionately and respectfully kissing it before he carefully began to unroll and read it. *"Thus says the Lord, the King of Israel, and his Redeemer, the Lord of Hosts,"* he forcefully said out loud, as though he were giving a recital to the attentive trees standing nearby, *"I am the First and I am the Last; besides Me there is no God."* (Isaiah 44:6) "Ah, pure truth," Paul joyfully commented.

The fog soon lifted and he was able to see sections of the town sprawled out before him. The reminiscing thoughts about his younger days soon dissipated and were crowded out of his mind by the recent events taking place in Lystra. Many fascinating things had happened since they arrived with the gospel message burning in their dedicated hearts. The Risen Lord had seen fit to confirm the validity of their words with quite a few dramatic miracles of healing. The most amazing of these was the healing of a person named Justus, a cripple who had never walked a day in his life. This man, who was born with hopelessly deformed feet, received faith to believe that this Jesus of Nazareth, whom Paul affirmed was risen from the dead, had the desire and ability to make him well. Paul had been granted supernatural discernment during an unusually powerful service one evening, somehow

16

knowing that Justus was going to be healed. Right in the middle of his sermon, Paul abruptly stopped preaching and then simply commanded Justus to stand up on his feet! When he immediately jumped up and began to leap around the room, some of the ecstatic first-time visitors ran out into the city streets, crying, *"The gods have come down to us in the likeness of men!"* (Acts 14:11) Paul had to laugh to himself as he thought back at how ridiculous it was for the townspeople to name him Mercury, and Barnabas, Jupiter. It took everything in them to restrain the people from sacrificing their choicest oxen to them. These people's minds were so taken up with reading silly books on Greek mythology that they actually thought Paul and Barnabas were gods!

That was only a few, short weeks ago. Now, a small, fledgling church was meeting nightly in their cottage. The excitement was still very high, and Paul was always careful to point the people to Christ, the Messiah. He joyfully worked hard, day and night, pouring out his soul to establish a congregation of believers who would carry on the message when he and Barnabas would be called to another city. As Paul looked over the small town he wondered how long it would be before the enemy would rise up his inevitable opposition to the work of God. As he began to fervently pray, these concerns, which burdened his heart, formed the requests he lifted up to his waiting Lord.

"Oh, Lord Jesus, keep these precious newborn believers from the Evil One. Help them to stand strong against the attacks of the enemy."

17

And then the Lord spoke to Paul's spirit. Not quite audibly but very clearly, the Lord said, "Paul, you will never forget this day which lies before you. I am with you. Be strong and very courageous."

Paul looked up into the sky, half expecting to see the bright Light from heaven he had encountered years ago. As he gazed upward, out of the corner of his eye, he noticed four or five dark shadows descending upon the center of town. Before he could make out exactly what it was, they vanished out of sight. "Lord," Paul whispered silently up to the invisible Throne of Grace before him, "only with Your help . . . can I be strong or courageous."

About an hour later Paul walked down the hill and back to the cottage, noticing, as he got closer, that smoke was billowing out from the chimney. As he entered the room, he was greeted with the sweet smell of cinnamon in the air. Barnabas had cooked a large pot of oatmeal, flavoring it with honey, raisins and cinnamon.

"Barnabas," Paul began, forgetting to even greet him, "have you ever seen demons?"

Barnabas thought real hard for a moment and then replied, "Only through the faces of the possessed. Why do you ask?"

"Oh, I don't know," he replied as he remembered the dark shadows he saw coming down upon the town.

After a short prayer of thanksgiving, they both ate a hearty breakfast and then immediately started praying in a time of earnestly worshipping their Risen Lord together. When they were done, they peacefully talked over their schedules for the day ahead of them.

Paul began by saying, "I need to finish the tent for Euclid today, if I can. I hope to give it to him tonight when he comes to the prayer meeting. We need to buy some food at the market and we also need to find some time this afternoon to go pray for Lois. She's been sick for a few days now. But she has so much faith. I'm sure the Lord will raise her up."

"Her spirit is so high, now that her grandson Timothy has given his heart to the Messiah," Barnabas added.

"Having a Jewish mom and a Greek father, you would think Timothy would have been a little bit more hesitant about deciding to follow Christ," Paul mused. "But he's one of the first and best converts here in Lystra."

"You know, Paul," Barnabas replied slowly and thoughtfully, "Timothy's mother informed me the other day that her son has memorized the entire books of Jeremiah and Isaiah. Because of the wonderful influence of his devout grandmother and mother, he has literally been studying the Scriptures since he was a toddler."

"Amazing," Paul said as he thought back to his own insatiable thirst for God's Word when he was Timothy's tender, young age. "I think there's a call upon his life to be a pastor," Paul continued. "He'll make a good leader, if he doesn't allow his timidity to get in the way."

"I agree that he surely has a call on his life," Barnabas stated emphatically. "However, it's definitely way too soon to tell him this. He doesn't need to overcome his shyness by becoming spiritually proud and arrogant."

"You're wrong," Paul suddenly blurted out. "Telling him he's called and special is just the thing he needs at this time in his life to boost his confidence."

"Paul, if he gets as puffed up as you were at his age, you'll be creating a monster, instead of a follower of Christ."

"A monster?" Paul retorted, being offended at Barnabas' way of describing his pre-conversion condition.

"Paul, if it wasn't for your deep-seated pride and insolent arrogance, you would have come to the Messiah years before you were knocked off your high horse on the road to Damascus. You know it's true," Barnabas chuckled.

"I'm going to the market," Paul abruptly said as he swung open the door and angrily walked out. He didn't slam it though. As mad as he was, he was hoping Barnabas would join him. Barnabas soon caught up to him and put his arm around his friend's shoulder, exclaiming, "I'm sorry, Paul. I shouldn't have said those things. Even when we disagree, I still love you, brother."

"I love you, too, and I'm sorry, also," Paul humbly replied as he also placed his arm on Barnabas' shoulder in return.

As the two men neared the town square, they heard what sounded like a crowd of people yelling and screaming. This was strange for a small town accustomed to extreme quiet, particularly in the early morning hours. Were they surprised at who they saw standing by the large granite columns in front of City Hall! The Jewish leaders from the two nearby towns, Antioch and Iconium! These men, upon hearing the undeniable reports of Justus' healing, secretly made their way into Lystra. Their goal was to first persuade a number of the influential Jewish citizens that Paul and Barnabas were dangerous heretics who performed miracles by the power of the devil! Once they gained a strong backing, their plan was to take their complaints to the streets. It was a subtle, underhanded strategy, but one that worked well when executed just right. They carefully instructed their supporters to casually walk past City Hall at that particular hour of the morning. As these unbelieving Jewish leaders began to speak out at the appointed time, the crowd swelled and the majority fervently agreed with everything they said. Their twenty or so followers incited and influenced the whole town with their cries, "The Christians must die! They are evil! Paul is a madman, who must be silenced!"

Both their hearts began pounding in their chests. One of the new believers, whose house was on a street a half a block from the town square, cracked open his front door and whispered as they walked by, "Paul! Barnabas! Hurry! Get in here!" Barnabas turned and silently jumped into the man's house, thinking Paul was right behind him. Once inside, he looked back, exclaiming, "Oh, no! Where's Paul?"

"I guess he didn't hear me," the brother said as he cautiously peeked out again.

Paul hadn't heard him. Neither had he seen Barnabas leap off the road into the safety of the brother's house. Paul kept walking, right towards the back of the crowd. The atmosphere on the streets was charged with intense, demonic hatred. Paul tried to shake off the fear that was gripping his heart and mind.

"What do you think we should do, Barnabas?" Paul nervously asked as he turned toward his companion, who was gone! Paul stopped short, hoping that he hadn't been seen. "Lord, what shall I do?" he softly whispered. "Should I run, should I try to calmly walk away before I'm seen, or should I stand up to these men and this crowd?"

The Lord's response came through Paul remembering God's word to him during his quiet time earlier in the morning: "I am with you. Be strong and very courageous."

At that moment one of the leaders from Antioch spotted Paul in the back of the crowd. "There he is!" he roared as he pointed his self-righteous finger right at Paul. "There's the heretic! Grab him!"

Before he knew it, a dozen or so hate-filled hands seized Paul and he found himself being dragged through the streets by an angry mob. He felt a constant barrage of punches, spit and kicks from all the aggravated people around him. "He must be killed! He must be killed," the people screamed in a satanically inspired frenzy. They pulled him a few hundred feet outside the city gates and then threw him to the ground as though he were a piece of filthy trash. By this time, hundreds of enraged men had surrounded him. He was trapped, and he knew it. It would be totally futile to try to run away now. No one in the crowd, even those who knew they were terribly wrong, had the courage to stand up in Paul's defense.

The leader of the group from Antioch took charge,

stepping forward and motioning with his left hand for everyone to listen. He was overshadowed by a shadow that no one noticed. He stooped down and picked up a jagged rock in his right hand, as others followed suit. This commander of the mob screamed at Paul, loud enough for everyone to hear, saying, "Would you like to recant of your heresies, or would you prefer to be stoned to death?"

Paul struggled to his feet with heaven-sent words still ringing in his dazed head: "Be very courageous. I am with you."

"Brethren," Paul boldly but respectfully began, addressing the many Jews in the mob as he attempted to wipe some of the dirt off his shirt. "I have done nothing worthy of death, as you all know. But to deny the truth would be a disgrace to the Messiah, and to my nation, both of which I love with all my heart. Like you, I once persecuted believers in Jesus, until the day that God spoke to me from heaven and said, *'Saul, Saul, why are you persecuting Me?'* When I replied, *'Who are You, Lord?'* *He said to me, 'I am Jesus of Nazareth, whom . . . "*

"Shut up, you evil deceiver!" the leader cried out as he threw his rock at him. The medium-sized rock hit the side of Paul's face and cut it open. The sight of blood awakened animal instincts within the mob, which then began to shower Paul with various sizes of rocks, pebbles, and sticks. As Paul noticed the blood dripping down the front of his shirt he tried to shield his face with his arms.

"Oh, Lord," he cried out from the depths of his soul, "I do long to be with You, but there's so much more work to do down here."

23

Just then, another rock struck his chest and violently knocked him to the ground, as the twisted crowd cheered at the direct hit to their target. Paul turned over and got on his hands and knees, noticing the pool of his blood quickly collecting underneath him. He suddenly had an overwhelming desire to run for it, for he knew his life was slipping away. He was dying. "Oh, Lord . . . may Your name be glorified in my death, as I have endeavored to glorify You in my life." Instantly, he was filled with grace, compassion, and pity for his blind, lost persecutors. As the rocks and sticks kept pelting his body, he clasped his blood-soaked hands together in prayer. He knew no one could possibly hear him, but at least they could see he would choose to leave this world interceding on their behalf, just as Jesus had, and Stephen after him, the first martyr of the church. By the time the last man threw his stone, the Apostle's dead body was almost totally covered with blood, rocks, sticks and stones. No movement was visible underneath it. As the contented mob stood there gloating, an unusually evil, demon-possessed man walked forward, carrying a large boulder in his arms. His mouth drooled like a rabid dog. His shadowy eyes were filled with hatred a million times more intense than normal human hatred could ever become. He grunted and growled and staggered over to Paul's body, having difficulty carrying such a huge load. He then dropped it right on top of Paul's skull, sounding an audible crack that everyone nearby could hear.

"That should do it," the man demonically laughed as he jumped up and down with hellish glee. The

24

deranged man looked so wicked, so evil, smiling and laughing over Paul's quiet, innocent body that it caused the mob to quickly turn away in disgust and disperse back into town. The man's behavior so clearly revealed the wickedness of what they had just done, that they were too uncomfortable to stay around and ponder their actions.

As everyone abruptly made their way back through the city gates, a lone, nervous believer immediately came out from behind a nearby house. And then another, and then some more. Barnabas cleared away the rocks and checked for a pulse that was long gone. One of the new believers wept profusely as he lifted the battered body out of the pile of rocks and into his trembling arms. Another disciple tried to wipe the blood out of Paul's eyes as though he still needed to see out from them. Another of the young converts, Timothy, cried in agony up to the heavens, "God, oh God, why would You allow such a horrible thing to happen to Your servant, Paul? Why?" Although Timothy was deeply distressed, there was also a hint of subtle pride in his voice, insinuating that God had done something wrong.

"Lay him back down," Barnabas lightly whispered. "Timothy," he gently added, "it's an honor to lay down one's life on behalf of the One who gladly did so for us all. Even so, let's gather around and pray. Perhaps the Father will raise him back to life as He did with sister Dorcas in Joppa." **(Acts 9:40)**

As the lifeless form of Paul's body was slowly laid back down upon the ground, the small band of dejected believers held hands, formed a circle around the dear

Apostle and fervently prayed to the God of Heaven.

TWO
CAUGHT UP INTO PARADISE

"I am with you," Jesus said, as Paul opened his glorified eyes and ascended into a new world. The voice of his beloved Savior instantly filled him with life and joy. His first thought was about the small band of disciples he had left behind, who had quickly gathered around his lifeless, earthly shell. He then turned toward where that lovely voice was coming from.

Jesus! Jesus of Nazareth . . . the personification of pure love and infinite power! The Messiah, shining with heavenly radiance, was holding out his nail-scarred right hand for Paul to take. The Apostle, however, fell to his knees, exclaiming, "Lord, I am so unworthy of Your mercy and grace."

Jesus stepped toward him, gently placing His hands on the weeping Apostle's bowed head. Paul felt eternal life and power and love and peace streaming into his being as definitely as water is poured into an empty glass, and as dramatically as a bolt of lightning splits apart the cedars of Lebanon. The Lord then helped him to his feet and gave him a hearty embrace as Paul wept with overwhelming wonder. Shoulder to shoulder they proceeded to walk through a long, dark tunnel ahead of them.

"*This* is the dreaded valley of the shadow of death?" Paul laughed to himself, as they continued.

The Lord, perceiving his thoughts, turned and smiled at his faithful servant, who was about to enter into the joy of his Lord. The light at the end seemed to be beckoning them to come and bask in the radiance of heavenly happiness. They came out on the other side into a beautiful, park-like world. Paul's mouth dropped open as his eyes went back and forth, taking in all the lovely sights, sounds, fragrances, and feelings of heaven. The first thing Paul was aware of as they entered into eternal Paradise was that heavenly worship music filled the atmosphere much like the air had covered the atmosphere on earth. The sound of angels' praise floated throughout the land, accompanied by the melodies of all kinds of lovely songbirds that were darting from tree to tree. Above the trees the sky was glowing with a bright, gentle radiance in this land of perpetual springtime. Paul looked down and realized he was clothed in a white, silk-like robe He noticed that flowers were growing everywhere. The grass underneath his feet had a noticeably deep, rich green color. Upon closer inspection he observed that every single blade looked perfect, beautiful, and seemingly woven together as meticulously as an expensive oriental rug. There was no hint of decay anywhere, everything being wonderfully alive, perfectly clean, looking as though just washed by summer showers. Fruit trees dotted the heavenly landscape; all of them loaded with exquisite blossoms or luscious fruits. Underneath these trees, many groups of happy children were laughing, playing, and jumping for joy.

In every direction people dressed in spotless white were casually walking, some in groups of two or three and some alone; but all of them exhibited an undeniable air of peacefulness and happiness, without a single care in their hearts. The ones near the Lord Jesus and Paul turned and waved a joyous welcome to Paul. The group that was closest turned and walked up to them. "Paul, my beloved son," one of them exclaimed.

"Dad, is that you?" Paul asked with amazement as he fell into his earthly father's opened arms. "And . . . Mother, Mother is that you? Oh, I'm so glad to see both of you," he said as he turned and hugged his mom, whom he hadn't seen since he was a teenager. "And, who is this?" Paul asked, as he politely caressed the happy face of a young woman who stood attentively, yet humbly nearby.

"This is one of your sisters," Paul's mom said. "Miriam died during childbirth, about two years before you were born. I was never able to talk about it; it was such a painful experience for me. But not any more," his Mom replied with fullness of joy. "This earthly daughter of mine has brought me so much delight since I arrived here in this land of Paradise," she gratefully added as she gave Miriam an affectionate squeeze. "And how is your other sister doing, Paul?"

"She's fine," he answered. "I was able to lead her to the Lord a few months ago. She's living in Jerusalem and being a great blessing to the church there."

"That's wonderful," his mom shouted out loud as she literally jumped for joy at such great news.

As Paul stared at his happy, healthy mother, the reality of heaven fell upon his soul and he bowed his head and began to weep again with deep gratitude. Jesus Christ, Paul's dad, mom and sister gathered closer to him, all hugging and squeezing him. A deep feeling of contentment, wholeness, and of "finally being home" swept through his soul like a peaceful tidal wave. He marveled at the thought that he had arrived at the place where there is no more sorrow, no more pain, no sickness or death. No disappointments, broken hopes, or mislaid plans! Nothing but light and joy, love and peace, forever! After a while, Paul regained his composure and wiped the tears off his face. "I always thought Heaven was a city," he said as he turned his curiosity-filled face to the Lord.

"This is just the outer edge of Paradise," Jesus lovingly answered. "Beyond that hill," he said as he pointed to the right, "is the road leading to the Holy City."

Paul looked to the horizon and could make out the top of what seemed to be a metropolis, way off in the distance. "It would take an entire day to hike that far," Paul thought out loud.

"Here in heaven," Jesus replied, "Mankind isn't confined to the things that hindered him while on earth. You can move about with ease, here." Suddenly Jesus, Paul, and his family were standing next to one of the pearly gates of the city. Paul looked up at the multi-colored wall and the huge gate of pearl with total awe. "Amazing!" he exclaimed, being more fascinated with what he was seeing, than how quickly they had arrived there.

"Perhaps we should go inside and show Paul his mansion," Miriam suggested with overwhelming excitement in her voice. They all looked into Jesus' face for direction. To the inhabitants of heaven, their joy is in doing the Lord's will in every matter, great or small.

"Well," Jesus tenderly began, "it still needs a little more work done on the back porch before it's completely finished. Why don't you all go and work on it and Paul and I will see you later on?"

"Sure," they all agreed as they proceeded to give long, affectionate hugs to both the Lord Jesus and Paul. They turned and walked into the city gates, singing and praising the Lord for His mercy that endures forever.

In an instant, Paul and his Lord were back in the outer regions of Paradise where they had been a few moments earlier. "Let's go this way," Jesus said as he darted up a small path leading up to a flowery hill. Paul followed him, running with tremendous ease and a deep thrill in his heart, realizing he now was enjoying perfect strength and total health. Paul started skipping, experiencing a level of delight he hadn't known since he was a happy boy in Tarsus. The path soon took them to a huge, architecturally perfect, Gothic mansion that had these letters artistically engraved over the front entrance: "NEW JERUSALEM LIBRARY, OUTER PARADISE BRANCH."

"A library?" Paul asked with childlike astonishment. Jesus laughed with joy as He opened the front door and gestured for Paul to enter before Him. Paul eagerly stepped inside, almost running right into a tall, radiant angel who had come to welcome them.

"Gabriel," Jesus cordially said, "Paul, the Apostle has arrived."

"Yes, I know," he joyfully replied. "It's a pleasure to finally get to formally meet you, Paul. I've seen you many times," Gabriel said as he warmly extended his angelic hand.

Paul's mouth hung open again, still wondering if this was all an incredible dream. Was he really with Jesus in heaven, in a library, meeting Gabriel?

"I'm going back to the gate to meet a few more new arrivals," Jesus began, speaking to Gabriel, His faithful, heavenly servant. "I'll be back in a little while to pick Paul up. Could you show him a book or two while I'm gone?"

"Certainly," Gabriel said with a huge smile. "I'll be glad to give him a tour." He put his arm around Paul's shoulder and began to escort him into the main room.

Paul looked back towards the Lord who was smiling at him with holy love. Oh, that look! So full of tenderness and encouragement. It lifted Paul and enthralled him. Jesus slowly nodded His head in assurance and then proceeded out the door.

"A heavenly library!" Paul exclaimed as he remembered all the wonderful times he spent in libraries ever since he was a child. As he looked around, he realized this library was like none he had ever seen before. Yes, the walls were lined with row upon row of books. But here, the ceiling was made of clear, transparent crystal, and the floors were covered with light green moss and many beautiful, multi-colored rocks. Marble columns graced the interior as well as the exterior of the building. Lovely trees and plants filled the spacious rooms, and yet it didn't feel crowded. There was even a small stream delicately flowing through the center of the huge room, enhancing the atmosphere with mild, forest-like background sounds. Paul slowly walked into this room, holding his breath with sheer joy and elation.

"Just look at all these tall books," he said out loud.

"Well, they're not exactly books," Gabriel answered. "They're more like doors. Instead of reading them, you enter in and experience them. For example," he continued as he made his way to the far wall, "in this section labeled Genesis, notice this book entitled 'The Creation And Fall Of Mankind.' Jesus took this particular book to the Tabernacle in the Wilderness and Moses was allowed to actually enter into it and experience it." The tall angel slid the seven-foot door out from the wall to show Paul the doorknob on the side. "This is how Moses could write the book of Genesis as an eye-witness. Through this door he entered into the past and was literally there as God created man and woman; and as the serpent beguiled Adam's wife, Eve."

"Incredible!" Paul exclaimed. He cracked open the door and looked inside. Everything was *"...without form and void, and darkness was on the face of the deep. And the Spirit of God was hovering over the face of the waters."* (Genesis 1:2)

"Are you certain this is one of the books you want to look at?" Gabriel asked. "King Jesus said you would probably only have time to look at one or two of them before He returns for you," he politely added.

"I'm not sure if this is the one I want to view," Paul said, as he backed out and carefully closed the door. "I've already read that one, so many, many times before.

Could I look around first and see what else you have before I decide?"

The angel smiled and nodded. Paul then made his way over to the mysteries section and glanced at some of the titles that were written on the sides of the book-doors. "THE MYSTERY OF THE GENTILE'S PLACE IN GOD'S PLAN OF REDEMPTION," he read out loud with a tone of intense interest. "WHY THE SNOW OF GOD'S GRACE ONLY STICKS ON CERTAIN HEARTS . . . THE MYSTERY OF MARRIAGE . . . THE MYSTERIES THAT MORTAL MEN CANNOT GRASP." Paul carefully pulled out the last title and looked inside. "Amazing! This is truly amazing!" He stood just inside the door and looked at things no mortal man had ever seen, or could ever grasp. **(2 Corinthians 12:4)** He stood transfixed upon the images projected in front of him.

"Paul," the angel politely interrupted, "this particular book is so deep it will take much too long for you to experience it all before the Lord returns for you. Perhaps you'd rather look at one of the shorter books in our theology section."

"Okay," Paul said as he stepped away from the opened door. "So, you have a theology section," he added.

"Yes, it's over here."

Paul began to read some of the titles aloud. "PREDESTINATION MADE SIMPLE . . . THE TRINITY EXPLAINED . . . THE END TIMES AND THE COMING OF THE LORD." He noticed this last book had some kind of lock or seal on it.

"Why is this one locked?" he asked.

"That particular one," Gabriel answered, "is reserved for the Apostle John during his upcoming vacation on the isle of Patmos. He's going to finish writing the Canon of Scripture with what he sees through that book-door."

"Oh," Paul simply said, with no trace of envy or jealousy whatsoever. He kept scanning the titles, and then he saw it. The title seemed to jump out at him. "THE ORIGIN OF EVIL."

"Can I see this one?" Paul respectfully, but eagerly asked.

"Sure," Gabriel said as he approached the door and slid it out from the wall. "Excellent choice, I might add. I'll go with you and begin the narration." Gabriel opened the book-door and stepped inside and Paul followed with the excitement of a child on Christmas morning.

THREE
BEFORE THE BEGINNING, THERE WAS LIGHT

Paul and the angel walked through the miraculous door into what appeared to be a vast space, filled with Light. Paul instantly realized they were standing on a small balcony that overlooked . . . nothing. At least nothing he could see. There were two cozy-looking chairs in the middle of this balcony, into which they soon made themselves comfortable. Paul was going to start asking a number of questions that were coming to his inquisitive mind. He refrained himself when he looked over at Gabriel's majestic countenance. He could tell from the look on his face that the angel was about to speak. Gabriel motioned for Paul to focus in on what was out in the distance.

As Paul obediently leaned back in his chair and attentively looked in front of him, he noticed an immense body of Light. Actually, there were three Lights, three enormous Luminaries, swirling around each other, similar to how a circus performer would juggle three objects in the air. It was even more than that. It was like a fiery wheel, with another spinning wheel within that wheel, and a third wheel within the wheel that was in the first wheel. And, at the same time, the wheels and lights looked more like persons than lights and wheels.

Then the angel stood up in reverence, and spoke; not with the cordial voice of a helpful librarian, but with a voice that was filled with heavenly authority:

"Before the beginning . . . there was Light; and the

Light was with God, and the Light was God. And there was no darkness anywhere, for God was all and in all; and there was, is, and always will be no darkness in Him; no, not even any shadows, no matter which way He turns." **(John 1:1,4; James 1:17)**

"And God had sweet, unbroken fellowship with God . . . God the Father, God the Son, and God the Holy Spirit."

The angel then abruptly stopped speaking and sat down. Paul noticed the three figures were becoming more apparent, holding hands as they twirled around and around in sheer delight and total ecstasy. Then Paul heard God say to God, "Let us make three forms of beings, each one with the ability to embrace and reflect a different aspect of the Light. We shall create cherubim, who in perfect innocence shall embrace and reflect the purity of the Light of God. We shall then create angels, who in choosing to worship God in the beauty of holiness shall embrace and reflect the purity and holiness of the Light of God. We shall then create mankind, who shall begin in innocence and then in choosing to receive Our redemptive grace shall embrace and reflect the purity, holiness, and the love of the Light of God."

Suddenly, babies popped into the sky from thin air. Well, not really babies—cherubim. They looked like baby angels with tiny wings. They soon learned how to use their wings and were flying around God's Throne like thousands of happy little butterflies just released from the cocoon of nothingness. Paul noticed how joyful, cute and innocent they all were.

God the Father and God the Son sat on the Throne of Glory, with the Holy Spirit hovering over the vast expanse of space. The Father thought, the Son declared it, and the Spirit energized the words into reality. "Let there be clouds and harps, heavenly hills and heavenly houses filled with all a little cherub's heart could ever want or need." Suddenly, the expanse was filled with clouds of glory, mansions of glory, harps of glory, and hills of glory. The cherubim flew around with glee; joyfully inspecting all the goodies their generous Creator was blessing them with. From far away these little creatures looked like a celestial cloud, a ring of twinkling stars swirling around the Throne. They were thus nicknamed, the stars of God.

The Pre-incarnate Son kept speaking heavenly things into existence as the Father kept thinking of ways to bless His new creation. The Lord soon leaned over to the Father and said, "The innocence of the Light of God is clearly manifested and reflected through these delightful creatures, Father. Shall we now cause Thy holiness to be expressed more openly?"

"Yes, We shall," the Father replied with ecstatic joy. "Let there be angels, angels, angels!"

In a moment of time, heaven was filled with thousands upon thousands of glistening angels. They all shone brightly with the countenance of God upon their faces. There was a transparency about them, allowing the Light of God to freely flow in and out of them without any hindrance. But they weren't yet holy; they were merely innocent. God then appointed the cherubim, who were perfect and unchangeable, to have a temporary place of authority over the angels, who were also created perfect, yet not altogether unchangeable. This arrangement would be revised at a set time in the future, when the angels would come into their fullness. The changeless cherubim were instantly and forever blessed with heavenly innocence. The angels however were created with a God-given free will, an ability to choose. They could not come into complete holiness until they recognized their free will and made the choice to embrace the holiness of God, thus reflecting that aspect of the Light.

All of a sudden, in one accord all the angels and cherubim fell on their faces, crying, "Holy, Holy, Holy is the Lord of the Heavenly Hosts! The heavens are filled with Thy glory!" They all stayed on their faces for a long time, crying out that phrase over and over. From the very depths of their hearts they expressed their gratitude to their Creator for the wonderful gift of existence. It caused Paul to get on his knees and join them in adoration to God, the Almighty Creator of all. He noticed Gabriel was also caught up in worshipping the Holy Trinity. After a while, all the celestial inhabitants took to their feet and then casually began flying around, meeting one another, and checking out the many and varied blessings of heaven.

The four angels who were closest to the Throne however, were too enraptured with God's holy presence to stop. They soon reached out and grasped one another's hands, somehow silently covenanting with each other that they would never, ever stop passionately worshipping Him who is worthy of eternal worship. To this day, those four living creatures can be heard, eternally saying, "Holy,

Holy, Holy, is the Lord of Hosts."

After a short season of exploration and fellowship, a sweet wind swept through heaven and in one accord all the angels once again fell on their faces and sang a holy song to their God and Maker.

"This is so beautiful," Paul said to Gabriel, who caught up in abandoned worship. A little while later, Gabriel rose to his feet and sat down in his chair. "This is so beautiful," Paul repeated.

"Yes, it is. I mean, yes it was," Gabriel said with a hint of sadness in his voice. "If only Lucifer had chosen differently," he added.

"Which one was Lucifer? I mean, which one is Lucifer?" Paul asked, remembering he was actually seeing the past in the present.

"See the tall, bright one over there, leading the choir?"

"Him?" Paul asked with astonishment. "But he's so beautiful, and dazzling, and anointed!"

"He, Michael, and I were especially endowed by our generous Creator. We were designated as archangels and formed three choirs to continually bless God with heavenly background worship music, even during the intervals of corporate worship."

"How sweet," Paul replied.

"Yes, it was very, very sweet. See, when everyone fellowships with one another, one third of us gathers around the Throne with our harps, violins and various other instruments. Lucifer, Michael and myself would take turns leading one of the choirs. It's Lucifer's turn right now."

Paul observantly stated, "It looks like each of you were endowed with an ability to reflect more of the Light of God's glory than the other angels."

"Yes, that's true. God made us that way. Notice how easy it is to spot the three choir leaders, each of us perfect in beauty, full of wisdom, and mighty in power. All three of us were anointed this way to better lead the others in worship. Such an awesome responsibility! After a while, those under each leader's care developed a strong bond with their respective choir director. This proved fatal to many under Lucifer's leadership."

"One fateful day," Gabriel continued, "the winds of worship swept through heaven, as it had done so a hundred times before. Only this time, something was different. Look and see for yourself," Gabriel said as he motioned towards the new scene before them.

Paul looked and once again saw all the angels fall down in one accord to worship the worthy God with total abandon; all except for one, lone angel who stayed on his feet. Lucifer just stood there, gazing around at all the other worshipping angels. That day Lucifer discovered his own will, like a baby who unexpectedly discovers his or her own feet. "I don't *have to* fall down and worship God," he realized. "I can choose to, and . . . I can choose . . . not to worship, if I don't want to," he said to himself, realizing he had uncovered something that was very profound, indeed!

As the angels around him sensed that the unity of the Spirit was disrupted, they began to open their eyes and look around; trying to figure out what had happened. They gasped in shock when they saw Lucifer just standing there. The bewilderment spread throughout the entire angel and cherubim congregation until everyone was staring at Lucifer, wondering what in heaven was he doing!

At that moment, God the Father stood to His feet and beckoned with His right hand for everyone to carefully listen. He spoke powerfully and yet, tenderly. "Lucifer," He began, "today you have grown to your fullest potential as an angel. You have discovered that I've placed within you the gift of will, a free will. No, you do not *have to* worship Me. Now, you are on the verge of something totally new. You're on the brink of complete holiness of heart. Today, you can give Me the highest worship that heaven has ever known . . . a worship that comes from a heart that chooses to worship Me, from an awakened free will."

"Or?" Lucifer questioned.

"Or, you can choose not to," the Father said with sadness in His voice.

At that moment Lucifer lifted up his arms, appearing to worship. He then abruptly lowered his opened hands to his chest; signaling to God with his body language, "Stay away from me." Suddenly, a large, steel-like wall appeared between God and Lucifer, depicting in the heavenly realm what was happening in Lucifer's heart. Every created being was baffled, dazed and confused. All the cherubim screamed in fear and ran over to the Throne, yelling, "Father, Father what is that?"

"That's . . . a wall," He answered. "A wall that Lucifer has just chosen to erect. Don't worry," He said. "It won't hurt you."

FOUR
THE REBELLION

Many of Lucifer's choir members were fascinated with his wall. They came over and examined every inch of it. "How did you do this?" they would constantly ask him.

"I just . . . decided to not worship God," he coldly replied with his arms crossed.

"But, how did you do that?" they would question. The other angels could not yet grasp the concept of choosing to not worship God. "But we've been created to worship," they would all comment. "If you stop worshipping God, then who or what are you going to worship in His place? You can't just stop worshipping altogether. It's part of your very nature. It's the purpose for which we were created!"

Lucifer didn't respond to most of their probing questions and statements because he did not yet know what he was going to do. He was like a child who suddenly realized he could choose to run away from home; but didn't know where to go. He was like a teenager who realized he could defy his parents . . . if he wanted to, but wasn't quite sure if he really wanted to go in that direction.

Soon thereafter, Michael and Gabriel grasped the reality of their free wills. It happened simultaneously with them. The winds of worship began to blow, triggering the usual response of everyone falling to their faces in worship. This time Michael and Gabriel simply stood on their feet, not moving an inch, as the awareness of their ability to choose dawned upon their young spirits. They looked over at one another, hoping the other would choose the right thing. They flew over to each other, meeting in the middle; their holy smiles revealing their decisions. They put their arms around each other's shoulders and lifted up their angelic voices in one accord. "God Almighty, we choose to worship You and You alone, forever and ever, with all that is within us!" Their worship immediately got deeper and sweeter as they embraced and reflected with all their wills the holiness of their God. Most of the angels wanted this deeper and sweeter communion with God the Father, Son, and Holy Spirit and they began to gravitate towards Michael and Gabriel's choirs. But there were some who were more fascinated with Lucifer's wall. "You know what," they would say to one another as they flew around it like bees to a hive, examining it from every angle, "this is the only thing that God didn't directly create!"

The winds of worship blew through the heavens once again. Everyone fell down in complete worship; everyone except Lucifer. Once again, he just stood there with his arms crossed. Because of this, the wall began to expand. It soon turned into a room; actually a cube consisting of a ceiling, a floor, and three connected walls. Then a fourth wall began to emerge. But it was more than just another wall. It was something else that heaven had not yet seen before. It was a door! A door in the heart of Lucifer. A door capable of shutting out the omnipresent, eternal, all-pervasive Light. While the room was still just a wall, and then a number of walls, the Light of God's glory still flooded through, just as the summer sunshine permeates a glass patio.

God the Father came to Lucifer while he was standing there, lovingly trying to convince him to not shut the door of his heart on the Light. After the winds of worship passed, Lucifer walked around his room, with the Father pursuing him.

"Lucifer," the All-knowing Father tenderly began, "it's best for you to turn your heart back towards Me."

"You can't force me, can you?" Lucifer replied to the gentle, yet firm warnings of God.

"No, I won't. But My love for you can't help but sternly warn you. To block out the Light would be wrong, and the consequences would be disastrous. You're getting dangerously close to the point of no return. Remember this, my dear Lucifer. Crossing the line into willful rebellion is an eternal decision, because there will be no possible chance of turning back for you then."

Lucifer began to cut these walks short, turning away and flying back to his ever-increasing box-room, as the Father, the Son and the Spirit began to weep for him in their hearts. Any careful observer could sense where he was heading, just from the tone of Lucifer's remarks to Father God.

Paul looked out into the distance, noticing that the walks between Lucifer and the Heavenly Father were getting shorter and shorter, always because Lucifer would cut them short. Then he saw that right when the Father was about to lovingly place his hand on Lucifer's shoulder at the very beginning of one of their walks, the angel turned away and abruptly stormed back into his room. A tense feeling permeated all of heaven. There was a deep sense that catastrophe was right around the corner, although no one knew what a catastrophe was, having never experienced one.

Paul jumped to his feet, and leaned over the balcony's railing, his heart pounding with fear and anxiety over the scene in front of him. He turned to Gabriel, who by this time was standing next to him. "Why doesn't the Father stop him?" Paul asked with deep tension seeping through his quivering voice. "Why didn't He prevent Lucifer from making his catastrophic mistake?"

"He tried. But Lucifer wouldn't listen," Gabriel mournfully answered.

"In view of all the destruction to come, why didn't God make Lucifer listen to Him?"

"God chose to give us a free will, Paul. Otherwise, any obedience, faith, or love we might show Him would be forced, and therefore not be genuine at all. We then would never be able to embrace and reflect His holiness or His love. Any created being not given the ability to choose between right and wrong is incapable of freely doing what's morally right. He is then not a free spirit but a machine."

"But the anguish and heartache caused by our decisions," Paul said in agony of soul. "Oh, why did God give us such power? He knew the destruction that Lucifer's, Adam's, and then mankind's decisions would cause!"

Gabriel lovingly continued, "The all-wise, all-knowing God decided it was good to create beings with an ability to act independently of His will and have the choice to reject or obey Him. If you were to compel beings to act morally correct, you override their free will. By granting them free moral agency, you concede the possibility that someone at some time might act in an evil manner."

"Is such an achievement worth the horrible cost? Could not God secure the same ends without these means?" Paul asked, being reminded of all the evil he witnessed on earth.

"God, in His perfect wisdom, created the best of all possible worlds. If it had been created in any other way it would have been less than the best of all possibilities. It's only in a universe where the horrors of war and slavery *might* happen, that the learning of self-sacrifice and valiancy and love *can* happen. If God were to have completely suppressed the possibility of moral evil *He* would be doing evil, for He would prefer the worse to the better. He would have then preferred to create a world where no one but He could truly love, no one but Himself would be able to truly live, in the fullest sense of the word. That would have been selfish and evil, and it's impossible for God to lie or to ever commit any iniquity." **(Titus1:2, Deuteronomy 32:4)**

"So then, if all this is true, and I know it is," Paul said with a faint, yet repentant smile, "then where exactly did evil come from?"

"There!" Gabriel said as he leaned over the balcony, pointing to Lucifer as he was hastily flying back

49

to his walls.

It wasn't long after this that Lucifer reached his right arm out from his walls and slowly, defiantly and willfully closed the door and the Light was banished from his heart. At that instant, a jolting heavenquake rocked the entire universe. All the angels and cherubim were badly shaken up from the unusual quake. They looked over in the direction of Lucifer, from where the heaven-shattering noise had originated. He was now hidden from view, hidden from the Light! His decision of choosing un-Light produced something that had never existed, up to that point—spiritual darkness.

All of the other created beings shuddered in an emotional fright that no one had ever experienced before. No one knew why they felt so bad . . . no one except for God. The Father, Son, and Holy Spirit huddled in a tight circle, interlocking their arms as they wept with each other and consoled one another.

"Darkness has entered," the Holy Spirit whispered.

"He has made his choice," said the Son.

"It was in his God-given power to choose," the Father added. "The choice must stand, because it was a genuine, willful choice. Michael and Gabriel's choices have brought them into holiness. Their choices shall stand, also."

As the door closed, Lucifer felt an exhilarating fear; fear of the unknown, and at the same time, it was accompanied with excitement over being a pioneer in a new field. This completely closed door created a vacuum of nothingness. No Light could enter, nor could love or life enter either. Spiritual darkness was born.

For a few moments all Lucifer could see was the thick darkness in front of him. He nervously looked and felt around the insides of his darkened heart. The walls were no longer transparent; no longer receiving and reflecting God's glorious Light of holiness. Soon, his eyes adjusted to this new, amazing darkness. He then realized the walls had turned into mirrors! Nothing but mirrors! He couldn't see out. All he could see was himself. And no one, except for God Himself, could look inside.

Lucifer slowly walked over to these mirrored walls, fascinated by what he saw before him. For the first time in his existence he saw his own face. He had always been able to behold the faces of the Father, the Son, the Holy Spirit, the cherubim, and all the other angels; but never his own face. Now, in this new place of isolation and nothingness, his appearance was all he could see. He opened and closed his mouth, staring with dangerous fascination at his own image being perfectly reflected on the wall in front of him. He placed his right hand up to the mirrors, wondering if he could also feel as well as see his own reflection. As Lucifer gazed upon himself, he noticed that he was literally glowing in the darkness, and glowing brightly! The anointing that God placed on him as a worship leader had surely created a beautiful radiance about him.

"Surely, I AM perfect in beauty," he remarked to himself as he turned his body slightly, admiring in the mirrors his physique, his face, and his angelic wings. "Surely, I AM the personification of wisdom." The darkness seeped deeper and deeper into his mind. Because of his immense brightness, contrasted and overemphasized by the dark background, corruption entered into his once flawless wisdom. The corruption came in the form of Lucifer losing sight of the fact that his glory was merely a small reflection of God's eternal and infinite glory.

Right at that moment, the Holy Spirit gently whispered into the angel's heart room, "Michael and Gabriel have been blessed by Father God with the same glory as you."

He didn't want to hear that truth, though he knew it was totally true. He looked to his right where Michael usually could be seen, and all he saw was his own reflection. He looked to his left to get a glimpse of Gabriel, and still his eyes couldn't penetrate through the mirror walls. He knew they were just as anointed and bright as he, but for a brief instant he chose to deny that truth, lest his worship of self be interrupted. His choice of shutting the door had produced a vacuum inside his heart where spiritual rust was able to form. It quickly spread to his mind and heart.

"I AM beautiful," he exclaimed out loud to the mirror images of himself as he continued pouring out self-worship. "I AM perfect. I AM therefore worthy of worship." Iniquity in the form of pride, which was conceived when the wall went up, was now birthed within his darkened understanding. He chose to arrogantly praise himself instead of praising the One who had lovingly bestowed such beauty and wisdom upon him. The deranged angel at that moment became the father of pride, birthing the original sin within the womb of his self-made darkness. He would soon become the father of lies, rebellion, and hatred, too. Before reaching his final destination he would become the father of a million other vices, including murder, lust, and war.

Suddenly, an irritating noise disturbed Lucifer's self-worship session. He soon realized that someone was knocking on his door. A shining cherub innocently and patiently stood outside.

"It's time for you to lead the next worship service, sir," he stated as Lucifer opened the door.

"I'm not coming," Lucifer flatly stated. "I don't have to worship God any longer, and I'm not going to!"

"That's not the point," the cherub innocently remarked. "We don't *have to*, we *get to* worship the Almighty."

Lucifer defiantly folded his hands together; his body language speaking loudly that he wasn't going to budge.

"Come along," the cherub cheerfully insisted. "Remember, the Father has placed us cherubim in authority over you angels; so please obey me."

A new emotion—anger—arose in Lucifer's heart. He violently slammed the door in the perplexed cherub's face.

"It's not right," Lucifer screamed. "It's not right! A perfectly wise, fully developed angel such as I having to submit to the likes of these dumb cherubim. This must change," he decided as he began pacing back and forth in his dark, expanding room.

Lucifer then opened the door and rushed to the Throne of God the Father. "Father, I must speak with you, right away!"

"Lucifer, why are you so uptight? Have you . . ."

"Father," he interrupted, "I AM perfect in beauty, am I not?"

"Yes, Lucifer, you are. Because I made you so. But who told you that you are perfect in beauty?"

"Never mind that," he exclaimed. "Father, I AM anointed to lead, am I not?"

"Yes, that is so," the Father replied.

"Then why in heaven have You placed those dumb cherubim in rank and authority above me?" he yelled.

Never, ever had God the Father been yelled at. The Father looked at Lucifer with eyes filled with love, pity, and authority. "Lucifer," He gently began, "these cherubim have grown as far as they can grow. But as for the angels, only yourself, Michael and Gabriel have awakened into your fullness. The rest of them have yet to grasp the reality of their free wills. Once they do, then I will reassign positions of authority . . . *as I deem appropriate.* If you choose to continue along the path you are going . . . "

Lucifer rudely darted away in anger, not even waiting to hear the Father's tender warnings. He flew into his darkroom to sulk. As his eyes adjusted to the darkness, he realized he wasn't glowing nearly as much as he had been earlier. Without a doubt, his brightness was only a borrowed reflection of God's glory, which was quickly starting to fade. He decided to simply ignore that truth as he proceeded to admire himself again in his many mirrors. He then chose to reject truth altogether. As he did, another quake rocked the heavens. Truth itself was being denied. Never before had truth been attacked or rejected. When nothing but Light had permeated the universe and filled every created being, there was no room for anything but truth. But now that darkness had been birthed in the heart of Lucifer, things were quickly changing. Lucifer decided to not abide in truth whenever any truths would interfere with his wishes. In the place where love of the truth had once dwelt, a devious plot began to emerge, filling his supernatural, intelligent, but twisted mind.

A little while later, Lucifer approached the Holy Throne of Glory with evil intent in his heart. It appeared to the angels and cherubim around him that he was worshipping God along with them, but God could discern that he had ulterior motives. (Sometimes, only the eyes of God can detect the heart of a hypocrite and the soul of a Judas.) Lucifer noted that the four angels who were right next to the Throne were also the ones who were shining the brightest. They looked like fiery creatures, actual flames of fire. All the angels who were privileged to dwell that close to the Throne would eventually become like brilliant flames of fire, he realized. Seraphim, fiery ones, they would be called.

Lucifer got as close to the Throne of Glory as he possibly could, not to be closer to the One worthy of worship, but to capture as many rays of glory that his being could hold. He thus lowered the act of holy worship down to the level of a lust-filled, naked adulteress sunbathing on a beach just to become more attractive to her susceptible victims. Right when the amount of anointing and glory upon him was about to cause his very being to explode, Lucifer suddenly flew over to a distant cloud, just in time to lead his choir. He chuckled inside as he began to lead the worship, realizing he had timed it perfectly. He still sang the same songs with all the right words and melodies, but something was definitely wrong. He was shining so brightly that his radiance kept distracting the angels in the front, hindering them from worshipping the God they were singing about. From where they stood, Lucifer seemed to be shining even brighter than God Himself! He was well aware of the fact that this wasn't true. He knew this was an illusion, but it fooled many of the innocent angels. Lucifer now definitely shone brighter than Michael and Gabriel put together. Michael flew over to Lucifer's choir to see what was going on.

"You're not leading these angels in worship to God," Michael remarked. "As a matter of fact, many of them are more mesmerized with your brilliance than with the One who gave it to you."

"Good!" Lucifer sang back with immaculate harmony, not missing a beat. "It's about time," he continued singing his reply, "that they realize they don't *have to* worship Him."

Michael flew away, his mind spinning with perplexity. He realized Lucifer had spoken truth, but there was something else mixed in with it: un-truth, or un-light, or some kind of foreign substance he had never heard or seen before. A lack of a heavenly motive was now in Lucifer's distorted song. Something just wasn't right, but Michael couldn't put his finger on it, having never been exposed to words coming from a darkened heart, filled with secret motives.

At the end of this worship session many of the curious angels gathered around Lucifer to chat with him. "How did you get so bright?" almost all of them would ask.

"If you think this is bright, you haven't seen anything yet! Come to my room with me and then you'll see how I glow in the un-light!"

Many of the angels allowed their curiosity to get the best of them, wondering what in heaven was un-light. About half of all the heavenly hosts found themselves crowding into the darkroom of the heart of Lucifer. As more and more angels entered, the room enlarged itself to accommodate them. Lucifer instructed the crowd to wait inside and he would be back soon. As the angels slowly and carefully made their way in, they sat down on the floor and waited. Once the door was closed it became quite dark inside. Lucifer quickly and secretly flew back to the Throne of God. He stepped right up to the front where the four seraphim were and then braced himself as he held onto two of their arms. The fire of God's glory fell upon him with wave after wave of brilliance. When he was literally burning with the brightness of lightning he darted away and soared right into his darkroom. His reflection beaming off the mirror walls created the illusion of a huge cosmic explosion of brilliance. Against the background of darkness, Lucifer surely looked brighter than even God Himself! Neither the Father nor the Son had ever looked so dazzling in the eyes of these angels! The effect was one of shock, bewilderment, amazement and then adoration. One thing for sure: Lucifer had their attention!

"The reason why I shine so brightly," he began his carefully thought out lecture, "is that I have come to realize that I do not have to worship God. I have a free will and can choose to not worship. As a matter of fact, the less I worship Him, the more I shine. You should be living up to your greater brightness, too." As these angels listened to him, darkness began to descend upon their hearts, also.

Michael hadn't followed the crowd into the darkroom; but when his turn was up in leading his choir he just had to fly over to the entrance and crack open the door. He quietly stood there, straining his ear to hear what was happening. He definitely didn't want to participate, but at the same time he felt he needed to find out what Lucifer was up to.

"You seem to shine even brighter than God Almighty," one of the angels in the front boldly remarked. Michael gasped with indignation upon hearing those misguided words. Most of the angels inside, however, heartily agreed with that statement, shaking their heads in unison as they looked around at one another.

Lucifer was waiting for this. He then said in his most authoritative tone, "God was as bright as I AM, at one time . . . when He first came into existence."

"Are you saying that God was created?" someone in the crowd asked aloud.

"Yes," Lucifer lied. "He wants us to believe that He wasn't created; that He is greater than us so He can rule over the universe without the danger of anyone questioning His authority."

"You're a liar," Michael said as he bravely swung open the door and walked into the room.

"And you're a weak servant; a puppet; a bound slave to an unjust Tyrant," Lucifer snapped back.

"To be bound to Him who is pure love, pure truth and pure joy, is not bondage but true freedom," Michael shot back without hesitation. "But, you Lucifer . . . you are becoming bound to unredeemable darkness if you think that you—a limited, created being—can successfully come against the Omnipotent God. How can the created lie about and argue against its Creator? You are a fraud, a blasphemous, proud and arrogant rebel. You're a contagious disease to all those who come near you."

Michael then turned and tenderly addressed the crowd of angels around him, compassionately looking into the eyes of his fellow beings. "He's a liar, my friends. You all need to get out of here before the darkness corrupts your heart as it has clearly corrupted his. You all had better follow me out now, while you still can." He marched out of the room with many of the bewildered angels following close behind him. Sadly, about a third of all the heavenly angels stayed to hear what else Lucifer had to say. As everyone had turned to listen to Michael's heartfelt plea, Lucifer subtly walked over to one of his most ardent supporters in the front row; an angel named Bee-elzeebub. He secretly whispered into his ear. "You shall become a prince when I come into the glory of my kingdom. I will reveal many secrets first to you, because you're so wise. For instance, a little while ago I overheard God say that the cherubim will always be in charge of the angels."

Lucifer flew back to the front and continued his propaganda as soon as Michael left. "The whole truth is, God wants us to obey Him without question so He can do whatever He wants, no matter if it's just or not. For instance, we all know that the cherubim are inferior to us. But have you ever noticed that their thrones are set higher than ours?"

At that moment, Bee-elzeebub unexpectedly felt compelled to tell a lie. All of a sudden he spoke up, loudly saying, "I overheard God say that the cherubim would always rule over the angels, no matter what anyone else thinks about it."

That seemed to be the spark that lit the fuse.

"You see what I mean!" Lucifer said emphatically. "You see what I mean! Proof that I speak the truth!" He was as convincing as he was conniving. His seeming eyewitness to the injustice of God convinced the unauthorized angel jury that, yes, God was guilty. Guilty of being unrighteous. Guilty of being unfair. All of the deceived angels began murmuring, talking and then yelling about how terrible God was for being such a tyrant. When the mob reached the height of emotional fury, Lucifer began spewing out more venom and lies.

"It's time to show God that He isn't the only One who should be making the decisions around here. Since I AM like God in the perfection of wisdom and beauty, then I should be like God when it comes to deciding positions of authority. God says the cherubim are to be over me. I say, my throne should definitely and immediately be above the stars of God."

"Yes," the deluded crowd cried out as one.

"I will set my throne on the sides of the north, above the stars of God, and I will be like the Most High!"

"Yes, that's the way it should be," Lucifer's followers chanted.

"And those of you," Lucifer continued, "who are wise enough to realize that I speak the truth, you too shall be promoted when I come into my glory."

The crowd then lifted Lucifer upon their shoulders chanting, "Long live co-king Lucifer! Long live co-god Lucifer, the anointed light-bearer. The one who shines like God! The one who is perfect in beauty and full of wisdom!"

The enormous crowd of angels followed Lucifer as he directed the ones carrying him on their shoulders. They resembled a huge swarm of locusts moving back and forth like a serpent in water. Hundreds of them carried the darkroom wherever their leader would take them. Their commander led them far away from the Throne, farther than any of them had ever gone before. They could never go beyond the reach of God's hearing and sight, however. Lucifer's motive was to get beyond the immediate view of all the other angels and cherubim. Lucifer then began unveiling his dark plans to the crowd of angels around him.

"Here's what we must do. I will appoint myself above the stars of God. I will set my throne above the cloud of cherubim. I will be like the Most High. I'm sure God will pose some resistance to our plan, but it's high time to let Him know we will no longer allow Him to have His way in every single decision. It's just not right."

"Yeah! That's right," they all screamed. "Let's put God in His place. That filthy, rotten Tyrant's days of ruling over us is coming to an end! We shall be our own lords, and eat the fruit of our own choices for ourselves; not His choices for us," they all exclaimed.

Lucifer's group then lifted up this room of darkness and he sat on top of it like a king riding into battle. He opened his mouth and began singing anointed, heavenly melodies with an absolutely beautiful voice. The rest of his angels soon learned the new worship song and they all accompanied him as he sang, "God lives, and so do I. God makes decisions, and so shall I. God decides what is best, and so shall I, for I AM, I AM, I AM like Him in wisdom and beauty." They all rose higher and higher into the sky, and then they turned in the direction of the ring of cherubim around God's Holy Throne.

"Where are you going with that box?" the chief cherub said to Lucifer as the other cherubim curiously flew near to see what was going on.

Lucifer hesitated for a moment, giving enough time for his army to gather around behind him. Then he spoke.

"I am, at this moment, appointing myself above you dumb cherubim," he snarled.

"But, Lucifer, wait," said the innocent cherub in the front. "We all know you angels are greater in power and glory than us little cherubim. And I'm sure that soon God will appoint you above us all. But you must wait on God's timing. Otherwise you will be, you will be . . . rebelling against God, and you will not succeed! It would be total insanity to not recognize how useless it is to even consider fighting against . . . Omnipotence!"

Lucifer's crowd all stepped back a few feet, being deeply affected by the reality of those sincere, truth-filled words. The main thing that came to Lucifer's darkened mind was the realization that he would have to do something quickly, or he might lose his vast and devoted following. Suddenly, a line began to appear in front of Lucifer, being drawn by an invisible hand. This line was made up of one word written over and over: REBELLION, REBELLION, REBELLION.

The chief cherub bravely repeated his last statements. "Soon God will appoint you angels above us. But you must wait on God's timing. Otherwise you will be rebelling against God, and you will not succeed."

Lucifer took a step forward, crossing over the divine line; a move only he and God knew the significance of. He abruptly reached out his right hand and grabbed the startled cherub by the throat, digging his nails into his skin. He then yelled into his stunned, baby-like face, "You're going to teach me? I'll show you who's going to succeed!"

The helpless, little cherub screamed and wiggled, but it did no good. As the other cherubim looked on in total shock and dismay, Lucifer proceeded to rip the poor little fellow apart, literally limb from limb. He first tore his arms off and tossed them into the air, smiling with hellish glee. Then he severed his tiny wings and legs like a deranged boy would torment a helpless moth. A thrill pulsated through Lucifer's being as he became enthralled with the pleasure of his own decisive, depraved, wicked act. He cast the poor, innocent, limbless body as far as his supernatural arm could throw.

Lucifer then ran into the crowd of terrified cherubim, yelling out to his group, "Let's charge the enemies and defeat them. Don't let any of them get away."

Some enemies they were! They were so frightened that most of them could hardly even move, much less fight! A few of them managed to fly away, but the rest of them just stood there, shaking in terror as the angelic army followed their leader in mercilessly ripping them apart, limb from limb. A small percentage of Lucifer's angels were so sickened by the senseless violence that they, at the last minute, decided against following his cruel rebellion. However, the ones who stayed were suddenly transformed into creatures with evil natures and bizarre appearances. As they fought the helpless cherubim, pure hatred streamed into their heavenly beings. Their chosen pride and rebellion burst forth poisons into their hearts, much as a ruptured appendix could fatally affect a sickly, human body. Bumps and spikes and all types of disfigurements instantly appeared on their heads, bodies, and arms. Their faces lost their angelic beauty and took on the expression of the intense hatred they allowed to take over them. They turned into extremely grotesque snakes and lizard-like creatures. Most of them looked like half-angel, half-vipers! Others looked like deformed animals of various shapes and sizes. They all had, in a moment's time, turned into demons! Their self appointed leader's hatred toward God grew to the point that fire proceeded out of his mouth and nostrils.   Lucifer, the magnificently beautiful archangel, had turned into a huge, red dragon, a winged serpent, the Devil. His once splendid form developed scales, spikes, and reptilian skin. His face became the personification of arrogance, hatred, and wickedness. He grew a large tail that had the sting of an enraged scorpion at the end of it.

In the midst of the fighting, one of the largest of the cherubim ran over to his throne and bravely cried out, "I'm not leaving my place of authority unless God Almighty moves me!"

Lucifer cast his hate-filled eyes at him and breathed out a fiery stream of liquid cruelty as he headed toward him. The fiery hatred burned everything in its path, including the tail of one from his own army.

"Hey, Lucifer, watch what you're doing," he said as he grabbed and blew on his sore, smoking tail.

"Shut up, or I'll burn you to a crisp, also," he screamed. The wounded and shocked demon quickly realized there would be nothing but hatred and strife in the kingdom of darkness into which he just enlisted himself.

Lucifer proceeded over to the lone cherub sitting on his little seat of authority. By this time the cherub was standing up on his chair, looking more like a toddler playing in his high chair than a warrior resisting an invading army.

"One little cherub, who loves and trusts God," he loudly announced to Lucifer and his hosts, "is more powerful than you and your entire group!"

"Oh, yeah," Lucifer screamed out. "We'll see about that! With one breath of my almighty mouth I shall destroy you, and I shall rule over the cherubim and angels, forever." He stopped and bellowed out a demonic laugh. (The first time laughter was ever filled with malice and envy.) He then arrogantly added, "And if God doesn't like it, I'll burn *Him* to a crisp, too!"

He reared his long trunk back, leaning upon his tail like a cobra. He then took a slow, deep breath, intending on making the little fellow a heap of ashes in an instant of time.

All of a sudden, God the Father stood up from His Throne and declared with a loud voice to His entire creation, "STOP!" The effect was astounding. Every created thing heard and responded to His gentle, yet overwhelmingly powerful command. Every created thing fell down from the impact of His word. No one could move. No one could move an inch. Everything, everyone had to stop. The Son came over to the frozen scene along with His sorrowful Father. The Pre-incarnate Christ looked down at the great red dragon, stating, "You are no longer a light-bearer. You are a darkness-birther. You are

66

no longer a shining one, a morning star. You are no longer Lucifer. Your name and nature is now Satan, a rebel and an adversary of the Light. You have willfully rebelled against God, against Light and against truth, and you shall not prevail. It shall be said of you, *'How you are fallen from heaven, O Lucifer, son of the morning! How you are cut down to the ground, you who weakened the nations! For you have said in your heart: 'I will ascend into heaven, I will exalt my throne above the stars of God; I will also sit on the mount of the congregation on the farthest sides of the north; I will ascend above the heights of the clouds, I will be like the Most High.' Yet you shall be brought down to Sheol, to the lowest depths of the Pit.'"* (Isaiah 14:28)

The Father and Son turned and slowly walked away with sadness in their hearts. There was no fear or apprehension of the insane enemy. The Godhead knew Lucifer would one day try to deceive the world with the lie that good and evil are opposite and somewhat equal forces. Just another lie from the father of Lies. The Evil One, through God's all-seeing eyes, is a condemned criminal, living on borrowed time, a created being who turned from the Light, and became by his own choice, darkness. As darkness, the absence of light, is vanquished when the light is turned on, so Satan will be destroyed simply by the brightness of the Lord's coming. **(2 Thessalonians 2:8)**

At that very moment Lucifer could have been confined to eternal hell; but everything happens in its time. The dragon scrambled to his feet and frantically began to

67

flap his huge dragon wings to fly away. Before he got too far, he turned back around and grabbed his darkroom, throwing it on his back and disappearing into the farthest reaches of heaven.

His horde of demons followed closely behind him, looking like a huge swarm of irritated locusts. They all escaped into his darkroom like a bunch of scared bees retreating into their hive.

FIVE
LUCIFER'S EXPULSION

As Satan and his demonic army crowded back into his un-lit compartment, they immediately began to make plans to attack once again. "This time, let's go straight for the Throne," Bee-elzeebub bellowed out.

"Hey!" Satan screamed in anger, "Don't forget who's in charge here!" The furious dragon flung his gigantic tail around and struck Bee-elzeebub in the back with his stinger. Bee-elzeebub cried out in intense pain. Once he realized what had happened, he wisely began declaring, "Great is the red dragon, full of wisdom and . . . full of knowledge, and worthy of praise and worship." (He was going to say he was full of wisdom, *and* perfect in beauty, but not even Bee-elzeebub could stretch the truth that far.)

Satan chuckled out loud as he slowly pulled his stinger out of Bee-elzebub's pulsating back. "That'll teach you to usurp my authority, you little idiot," he added. "Anyone can see that I AM the only one wise enough to decide how and where to attack."

"Yes, Mighty One. Yes, Master," he wisely agreed.

"Does everyone else agree with me?" Satan asked his army as he proceeded to pour out an intimidating stream of fire from his mouth and nostrils.

"Oh, yes, Mighty One. Yes, Master," they all chanted as they fell to their knees in worship. (It wasn't the type of worship that flows out from the heart, but rather the kind that comes from the fear of being burned to a crisp.) Satan had become exactly the type of leader he had falsely accused God of being: a ruthless, cruel tyrant.

He gathered his troops around him and began to divulge the plans his perverted intelligence had cooked up.

"Our army is about half the size of theirs," Satan began. "So what we have to do is outsmart them. You all are aware of my superior intellect." He stopped for a second and blew himself a kiss in the mirror wall. "So, listen to me carefully, you half-wits. I have a momentous announcement. I've invented a secret weapon. It's called deception. It's a mixture of truth and lies, with a blur, as to which is which. Watch my deceptiveness," he said to his disciples.

"I AM an angel, I AM an angel, I AM an angel," he chanted over and over. As he did, he began to twirl around at a tremendous rate of speed. In an instant, he stopped turning, and all his onlookers stared at him with great surprise. Before them stood Lucifer, the shining angel, the one full of wisdom and perfect in beauty.

"I AM able to transform myself into what I was before. Don't I look just like an angel of light, and yet I AM the King of Darkness! I would rather be the Ruler over the Domain of Darkness than ever again bow my knees to that Tyrant of Light." His face was shining with the joy of hysteria. He was now drunk on his own arrogance and on his own delusions of power and glory; a false glory he had promised to share with those who followed him.

"Yes," his followers yelled. "Long live Lucifer!

Destruction to the Tyrant of Light!"

"Once you also learn how to transform yourselves back into angels, we shall deceive the angels that are around the Throne. We will tell them that God has appointed us to take their place just for a season. And once we are in place, we will attack the Tyrant's Throne together. With the angels out of the way, all of us collectively will have enough power to completely destroy Him." As strange as it may seem, he actually believed his irrational words.

The demons proceeded to follow their master's example and began twirling and chanting, "I AM an angel, I AM an angel, I AM an angel." Some of them caught on right away, while others had to work on it for a while to get the hang of it.

"Bee-elzeebub, come here," Satan demanded. The wounded demon reluctantly stopped twirling and scampered over to him, cowering in fear like an abused animal. "I have a project I want you to work on with me," the Prince of Darkness began. "We need to create what I will call . . . a grand illusion. Let me explain to you what I mean by that." He put his arm around his shoulder and walked away from the noise of all the demons who were practicing their chanting and twirling.

After a while, the box of darkness began to float, almost imperceptibly at first, closer and closer to the Throne of God. Once it was within clear view of the stars of cherubim and the hosts of angels, it mysteriously stopped advancing. Then, all of a sudden, a streak of light similar to a lightening bolt became visible to everyone. It seemed to have proceeded from the direction of the Throne. It struck the box of darkness with the impact of a million nuclear bombs. BAMMMM! In an instant, the box exploded into a trillion pieces, a ton of smoke, and a million loud screams. And then, silence. No smoke. No shattered pieces. No screams. Nothing.

All of the cherubim and angels looked at one another with huge eyes and open mouths. "What happened to Lucifer and his box?" they all asked one another. "What happened to all the angels who followed him in his rebellion?"

The impact of the lightning blast was so fierce that they were all reluctant to speak to God about it. "Apparently, God was very, very angry with them," one of the angels assumed. "He has annihilated them all, in the blink of an eye!"

"But how can you obliterate eternal beings such as angels," many of them mused.

"You saw the tears on God's face when He spoke to Lucifer," one of the little cherubim slowly uttered. "This was a very painful thing for God to do. It's best not to ask Him about it for a long time," he concluded as small tears flowed down his baby cheeks.

They all agreed with him. It definitely appeared best to not talk to God about it at all.

It wasn't long after this that one of the angels spotted a ring of lights about a trillion miles away, quickly getting brighter and brighter as it raced toward them at the speed of light. As the lights got closer, the innocent cherubim began to jump and dance around for joy.

"Look! More angels! It looks like God has created more angels to take the place of the evil ones that He obliterated!"

This new ring of angels came up to the others, asking the same type of questions that were once in their minds when they were first created. For these beings were not angels. They were the demons, all disguised in their former appearances, with a few alterations here and there to not arouse any suspicion.

"What are we called?" they innocently asked. "Where is our Creator? Why do we feel an urge to fall on our faces and worship Him?" The angels and cherubim had a delightful time teaching these seemingly new students the ABC's of heaven.

"When the winds of worship sweep through, let's all fall on our faces and sing hallelujahs to our Creator," Michael instructed.

Soon, the winds came and they all reverently fell on their faces, singing hallelujah over and over. Once the winds subsided, they arose and mingled with one another—newer angels questioning older angels, or so it seemed. One of the new angels shined just as brightly as Michael and Gabriel.

"My name is Reficul," Satan said to Michael, extending his arm for a warm handshake.

"Ref-i-cul." Michael repeated, not realizing it was the name Lucifer, spelled backwards.

"Yes, Reficul. Our wonderful, benevolent Creator told me that I was to be an archangel, like you. He also said that He was going to create one more batch of angels in the farthest reaches of heaven. All the older angels are to go and meet them out there. I'm not sure why," he added with an innocent smile. "But who are we to think we could understand all that the Great Creator does." He wanted to trick Michael into not even questioning God's unusual instructions given to new angels for the older ones to follow.

Suddenly, one of the inquisitive cherubim pointed his little finger up in the air, saying, "Look! *Another* ring of light! This is a great event! The Creator is making more and more angels! What a glorious moment this is," he exclaimed as he relived the joy he experienced when he was first created.

All the demons instructed the angels and cherubim to go and greet this newest batch of angels far away, in the farthest reaches of heaven. The angels and cherubim began taking off into the heavens like a happy group of obedient butterflies. The newer angels stayed near the Throne, about a hundred feet away, pretending that they were about to continue the worship services while the others were gone. Michael felt uneasy about this, but couldn't put his finger on why. Instead of flying off with the rest of the angels, however, he turned to Reficul and asked, "So, did God tell you *why* He decided to create more angels?"

"Uh, yeah, He did," Satan remarked, searching his vast intellect for a good, quick answer. "He said . . . He wanted to replace all those evil angels that He had to blow up."

"He mentioned the evil angels?" Michael asked

with bewilderment. "And He used the term, 'blow them up'?"

"Well, yeah," Satan declared as he decided to get away from Michael as fast as he could. "I've already said too much to that creep, that low-life, that slave to the Tyrant," he silently murmured to himself as he made his way into the middle of his camouflaged army. He then yelled out, "As soon as the next wind of worship subsides we all know what to do, don't we?" cueing his troops for their timely attack.

Everyone shook their heads in agreement.

Moments later, a fragrant breeze from the winds of worship began to blow and they all fell on their faces and began to sing sweet hallelujahs. Some of the other angels and cherubim who had also felt a bit uneasy about leaving the worship service in the hands of the newcomers began to feel peace about it as they observed their worship. One by one they flew away to join the group who was now well on their way to meeting the new arrivals.

But not Michael. He made his way right up to the Father's Throne. The Father leaned over to him saying, "My eyes can detect hypocrisy that is even unapparent to angels and cherubim."

"What are you referring to, Father?" Michael curiously and somewhat nervously asked.

"I did not create more angels."

"What?" Michael asked in shock.

The Father quickly placed His hand on Michael's arm, gesturing for him to calm down and keep quiet. Then the Father quietly and slowly whispered. "These worshipers before us . . . are not worshipers. They aren't even angels. They're the fallen angels; the demons, disguised as angels."

"I, I . . . was wondering about . . . "

"About the angel you were speaking with? That's Satan. He's about to attempt an attack on the Throne. It's so sad. He is now spiritually deranged and totally irrational. Then again, every sinful act is an expression of spiritual irrationality. But for him to stoop so low into darkness that he actually imagines that he has the ability to destroy Me! A creature coming against the Creator! The darkness within him has definitely reached the level of irredeemability. This time there will be found no darkroom for him to hide. He blew up his little darkroom, as part of his scheme to deceive the hosts of heaven. There will be found no place for him here in the heavens anymore."

Michael slowly shook his head up and down, signifying he was beginning to understand what was going on. "But they seem so sincere," he remarked as he looked out upon the vast crowd of thousands upon thousands of demons, all on their faces singing sweet but false hallelujahs to a God they were about to rise up against and attempt to destroy. Satan sang the loudest, singing the same worship songs, yet inwardly praising himself for accomplishing the immense task of converting so many of God's creatures into God-haters.

"Father, they sure look like they're really worshipping You!" Michael commented.

"Wait until you see how many hypocrites will lift

their voices in churches all over the Earth one day," God the Father remarked.

"Earth? Churches?" Michael asked. "What's a church?"

"Oh, it's something in the future that I'm reflecting on now as I look over the false group of worshipers before Me. Satan will one day be instrumental in corrupting the worship of beings on a place I will create and name Earth. Anyway. Let Us deal with what We have to deal with now. You, Michael, have been selected to cast the irredeemable enemies out of heaven."

Michael looked down at Satan, who appeared to be a perfectly beautiful and absolutely harmless angel of Light.

"How am I going to do this?" Michael humbly but confidently asked the Father.

"With the help of a weapon from My Son," the Father answered, as He looked over to the Pre-incarnate Christ sitting next to Him.

The Son of God stepped down from the Throne and walked over to Michael, saying, "The Words of God declare: *'Whosoever shall exalt himself shall be abased; and he that shall humble himself shall be exalted.'"* **(Matthew 23:12)**

These words streamed out of the Son's mouth in the form of a beam of Light, the shape of a sharp, two-edged Sword. The Son reached his hand to His mouth and grabbed the end of this Light beam. He then handed the Sword to Michael, saying, "This is the Sword of the Spirit, the Word of God."

77

Michael carefully reached out both hands and received the precious Sword from the Lord's hand.

"As you wield this Sword," the Son continued, "you will go in the might and strength of the Lord your God." The Son turned away; hiding the tears He was shedding over the horrible fate of Lucifer. Many, many tears had been shed over him, but these would be the last. It would be the last time that God would ever again weep for this self-corrupted, twisted being.

As soon as the worship began to die down Satan gave out a loud, ferocious roar, yelling, "Charge! Destroy the Tyrant!" As his army rose to their feet and came closer to the Throne of Truth, all hypocrisy had no choice but to go. They were instantly stripped of their costumes, transforming back into their ugly, demonic appearances.

The Father, Son, and Holy Spirit faced each other, speaking words of comfort and love to one another. They knew there was no danger whatsoever from the deluded, puny enemies. They didn't even want to watch the unmatched, unentertaining fight.

Michael flew out to the front of the Throne, holding the Sword of the Spirit in front of him. He lifted it up over his head, proclaiming, "These are the Eternal Words of the Almighty God: *'THE HUMBLE WILL BE EXALTED AND THE PROUD WILL BE ABASED.'"* **(from Matthew 23:12)**

Bee-elzeebub charged after him like a wild, angry bee. Michael was ready for him and quickly swung the Sword of Light in his direction. That was all it took. Bee-elzeebub was hit hard and went spinning and screeching into the far distance.

"Listen," Satan then cried out to his disorganized group. "Let's first surround him and then we'll all charge this Tyrant's weak slave from every direction." They all encircled and slowly closed in on him, looking like a pack of hungry, wild dogs. "You're surrounded, you weak slave," Satan chuckled with evil delight.

"I may be surrounded, and I may be weak," Michael admitted, "but my God has given me His Sword of infinite power, and you will not succeed."

Michael began swinging the Sword to the left, to the right, and then simultaneously began swinging it up and down. He quickly realized that as one begins to use this Sword, its infinite power starts to flow through its user, giving the ability to wield it in every direction at the same time. Soon, Michael couldn't even be seen. All the enemies could discern was a circular blade of Light and Power. It actually looked like a thousand circular saws in one, which had a thousand blades turning in each direction with infinite speed and almighty power. The circular saw approached the enemies as the words of God resounded from the blade: *THE HUMBLE WILL BE EXALTED, AND THE PROUD WILL BE ABASED.*

The demons stepped back in horror at such a sight. Only Satan was brave enough, or crazy enough, to hold his ground. He reached out his right hand to grab the archangel by the throat, as he had done earlier to the little cherub. The advancing, rotating blade touched the tips of his fingers, ripping them to shreds.

Satan fell down in sheer agony and terror. He

grabbed what was left of his right hand and held it to his chest, crying out in pain and hatred, "I hate You, God! I hate You!" His army then flew away in fright. Bee-elzeebub and a few other leaders came back, picked up their wounded commander, and scampered away. But there was no place for them to escape. They had blown up their dark box headquarters as part of their deceptive plot.

By this time the angels and cherubim arrived at the ring of light they had been deceived into thinking was a new batch of angels. From a distance it certainly looked that way. But as they got closer they realized it was nothing more than a cluster of mirrors, arranged in a large circle, facing the Throne of God. It was an illusion, merely reflecting the Light of the glory of God, as the moon reflects the sun. One of the first angels to arrive remembered seeing these mirrors in Satan's darkroom. He was one of those who followed Michael's advice and left before he was fatally corrupted. He knew right away that Satan was the one behind this deception, and was probably still around—somewhere.

"We've been deceived," he yelled out to all the arriving angels and cherubim. "This is the work of Lucifer. These are definitely his mirrors. We'd better get back to the Throne right away. Something's terribly wrong."

As they sped back to the Throne, what a sight met them! The Father, Son, and Holy Spirit were gathered into Oneness, with Their eyes closed in deep sorrow and shared grief. Thousands upon thousands of demons were running scared from a fiery, flaming Sword, which turned every way at the speed of light. The good angels returning to the Throne met the fleeing evil angels in mid-air. The angels grabbed the demons by their arms or tails or wings or spikes . . . anything they could get their hands on. The demons screamed and scratched and clawed, but the angels wouldn't let them go. Instinctively, they knew the right thing to do. The angels who weren't wrestling anyone gathered around, clasped their arms together and made a net to catch the fleeing demons.

Michael, the God-appointed leader in this battle, lowered his Sword down to his side and spoke directly to Satan. "I bind you in the authority of the name of the Lord God Almighty." Instantly, the great, red dragon was covered with chains from head to foot, or more precisely, from head to tail. The other angels followed suit, speaking words of divine judgment, which formed chains around the guilty criminals. After a while, every single demon was bound with these large, powerful chains. They screamed and shrieked, yelled and kicked. The harder they resisted, the tighter the chains dug into their skin.

God the Father lifted up His head and walked back to His majestic Throne. The Son followed Him. They were no longer crying. The tears were gone. A look of holy anger was upon Their majestic faces; anger at sin, anger at pride. Then the Father spoke. "Because of your choices, your violent actions, and your sinful rebellion, there is no longer a place for you in My Kingdom, Satan. Your destiny shall be a place called hell. Depart from Me, for you are cursed with the fruit of your own choices."

"I'd rather rule in hell than bow my knees to the

likes of You, You cruel Tyrant," Satan snapped back as he tried to shake his chained fists at the Holy Father. He then attempted to lunge forward toward the Throne, but was again restrained by the heavy chains that caused him to fall down. He somehow struggled back to his feet and faced the Father as all eyes were upon this strange looking sight. An angel of Light, bound with chains of darkness. A holy being filled with unholy hatred and malice! Satan then gathered up a disgusting lump of mucus from his sinful throat and spit at God with all his might. The thought of a created being actually attempting to spit in God's face was even a shock to the fallen angels. Every created being—angel, demon, and cherubim—turned and watched in disbelief as he dared to spit in his Creator's holy face.

The spittle would have landed right between God's eyes, had He not slightly turned His head. The filthy saliva flew past Him, behind Him, and then down, down, down it fell. All created eyes followed it as it descended. A rumbling sound began to be heard in the direction of Satan's spit. The heavens itself revolted at the thought of having to keep within its existence such an ungodly, unheavenly, and unholy thing as spit that was intended for the lovely face of God. At this point there was no other place for it to be, other than the heavens; for that was all that had, thus far, been created. Even so, heaven itself seemed to cough and gag and then painfully open itself up. The very place where the spit was heading began to scream and shake and roll up like a piece of used carpet, disclosing a horrible gap. Down in this unusual abyss was nothing but darkness. And into this darkness, this hole, this pit, the spit fell. The spit then grew and multiplied into a large lake of spittle, which filled every nook and cranny of this strange pit. As everyone stretched their necks to look upon this bizarre sight, this spit suddenly exploded into burning fire—a lake of burning fire. A place of darkness, pain, and fire. The fires of hell.

"You first," Michael declared as he grabbed Satan's chains and began to drag him to this God-forsaken pit.

"Noooo! Noooo! Stop," Satan screamed. Stop!"

No one felt sorry for him. None of the evil demons, holy angels, or innocent cherubim. Not even the Father of Mercy and Grace, or the Son of His Love. Satan's huge body was literally cast into the pit as the horrified demons helplessly looked on. As he was falling in, his massive tail reached out and grabbed on to the top of heaven's rim. Michael ran over to him, once again wielding his Sword over his head. **"The proud will be abased,"** he said with divine authority as his Sword struck Satan's tail. It cut the tip right off.

"Nooooooo!" Satan yelled as he fell headlong into the darkness. Michael picked up the tip of the tail and carefully examined its deadly stinger before tossing it into the pit. The rest of the demons, who were already bound in chains, resumed their squirming and screaming. They were each yanked, pulled, and then pushed to the edge of the ominous hole by one or two angels.

Like clockwork, the next tide of the winds of worship in heaven began to gently blow. All of the angels and cherubim instantly fell on their faces, forgetting about the enemy and the battle, as they unanimously joined in the most important, most blessed essence of their being— worship of their God. The bound enemies just stood there, chained and unable to move as they teetered on the brink of eternal expulsion. All of a sudden, the winds picked up dramatically. For everyone who was standing, the winds began to literally blow them away, towards the direction of the horrible pit. Upon evaluating the situation, the fallen angels realized that God seemed to be giving them one last chance. If they would merely fall on their faces before Him, in worship and repentance, the winds would apparently not sweep them into the abyss where Satan had just been hurled.

Bee-elzeebub turned in the direction of the now hurricane-force winds and yelled, "Not only will I not fall on my face in cowardly, vile prostration to the Tyrant, but neither will I ever again bow my knees to Him."

"That's right," all the rest of the evil angels declared, trying to scream over the sound of the gale-force winds. "We'd rather rule in the darkness with Satan, than to ever again submit to the Light!"

Suddenly, the winds intensified a hundred-fold. Swoosh! The sound of a mighty, rushing wind was heard, as of a mighty trumpet blast, sweeping them into the pit. Gone forever. One third of the angels, expelled from heaven forever and ever, along with their hideous leader. The moment the last remaining demon fell into the pit of hell, the gap closed up like an impatient elevator door.

The winds subsided and the angels and cherubim rose to their feet, noticing that the enemies were no more.

Even the gaping hole was gone. They all hugged and comforted one another for a long time.

Gabriel looked over at Paul who also needed some comfort. He put his hand on his drooping shoulders and whispered something so softly that Paul hardly made out the words. Gabriel spoke to him again, speaking a little louder this time. "Thus it shall be written in the Holy Scriptures: *'And there appeared another wonder in heaven; and behold a great red dragon . . . and his tail drew the third part of the stars of heaven . . . And there was war in heaven: Michael and his angels fought against the dragon; and the dragon fought and his angels, and prevailed not; neither was their place found any more in heaven. And the great dragon was cast out, that old serpent, called the Devil, and Satan, which deceiveth the whole world: he was cast out . . . and his angels were cast out with him.'"* (Revelation 12:3,4,7-9)

Gabriel then said to Paul, "We need to look at some more scenes before we leave this book."

They looked down and saw the angels ministering healing to all the cherubim who were still shaken up from being torn to pieces by Satan's army. "We sure are glad we were created cherubim and not angels," they said as their bodies and souls were being restored by the many angels who chose to not leave their assigned places. "Otherwise," they added, "we might have ended up like those awful, fallen angels."

Michael returned to his place near the Throne with a question burning in his heart. "Holy Father," he began, "I know everything You do is perfectly right and completely holy. If it seems otherwise to me, it's just my ignorance showing. Really. I know this is true. So, could You please explain why You said that Satan is going to have an influence upon Your soon-to-be-created Earth? Would it not be better for him and his evil ways to be eternally confined to the pit, where he rightfully belongs? Why allow him to continue spreading his evil influence?"

God the Father began very slowly. "Mankind will originally be created as innocent as cherubim and as free as angels, with the ability to stand against Satan's wicked influence. However, they will fall by their own free will. But even without the tempter around, all beings graced with a free will would eventually have to choose between Light and darkness. The angel's choice consisted of either remaining with or departing from the Light and going with darkness. Fallen mankind's choice will consist of either remaining with or departing from the darkness, and coming to the Light. Regardless of what Satan is allowed to do, or not to do, all free beings would eventually have to use their God-given freedom to choose between Light or darkness."

Michael developed a strange look on his face as his mind couldn't help but form another question. The All-knowing Father saw his unspoken question and remarked, "Michael, just because I can see beforehand what will take place, it doesn't take away from the genuine freedom to choose, which I have bestowed upon My creation. Foreknowledge does not always predetermine destiny. Otherwise the choices would not be real, and the freedom would not be genuine but a facade. Before the creation of mankind, even before I lay the foundation of the Earth, I will provide a way for fallen man to be redeemed, to come out of the evil darkness and into the marvelous Light of God. They will all fall into such a deep pit of sin that their spiritual blindness will render them completely incapable of even choosing to come to the Light."

"How then will they eventually choose the Light over darkness?" Michael curiously asked.

"Through My unmerited grace. I will pour My grace upon all mankind. I will draw all men to Myself. I will freely and graciously offer them the love of the truth. I will break the power of darkness off of them and in so doing, grant them the ability to choose or reject Me. Yes, Satan will be allowed to devise evil against My new creation, but I will turn it around for good. Even the power of evil itself could never go beyond the reaches of My Redemptive love and Light." The Father then slowly repeated the last sentence. "Even the power of evil itself could never go beyond the reaches of My Redemptive love and Light."

After that statement He paused for a moment, allowing its truth to sink into Michael's heart. Michael slowly began to nod his head up and down, signifying that he was beginning to understand.

The Father patiently continued. "I purposed a long, long time ago to create three types of beings. I declared to My Son, 'Let us make three forms of beings, each one with the ability to reflect a different aspect of Eternal Light. We shall create cherubim, who in perfect innocence shall embrace and reflect the purity of God. We shall then create angels, who in choosing to worship Me in the beauty of holiness shall embrace and reflect My holiness. We shall then create mankind, who through Our grace will be enabled to choose to receive Our redemptive grace, and thus embrace the love of God.'"

"Redemptive grace?" he angel questioned. "Redeemed from what?"

"Redeemed from the power of sin, the power of darkness, and the power of the devil."

Michael emphatically exclaimed, "That's going to take an amazing amount of grace!"

"Yes," the Father said. "It's going to take everything I have, and everything I am. And everything that is dear to Me," He added as He glanced over to His Son, the Pre-incarnate Christ.

"Without a doubt," Michael added, "those redeemed humans are really going to love You."

"Yes, the ones who will allow Me to redeem them will. They will receive and reflect My love just as you reflect My holiness, and as the cherubim reflect My innocence. I will so love the inhabitants of the world to come, that I will give them My only non-adopted, eternal Son, so that *whosoever believes in Him will not perish, but have everlasting life.* I will not send My Son into the world to condemn the fallen world, but so that they might be saved. Whoever chooses to believe, trust in and rely upon Him and His sacrificial death as the price paid for their salvation will not be condemned; but whoever refuses to believe will be condemned. And this is the grounds for the condemnation of those who choose to not believe: That Light will come into the darkened world, and those who decide to not come to the Light will do so because they would rather hold on to their dark, evil ways." **(From John 3:16-20)**

SIX
WHAT DRIVES HIM?

The Light began to fade and Paul supposed the book was over. He rose quickly, realizing that in a few more minutes it would be too dark to even see their way back to the library entrance. Extremely thick darkness was rapidly falling upon them.

Gabriel grabbed Paul's arm, soberly announcing, "Sit down, Paul. You must learn three things about the enemy before we leave this balcony. It is bestowed upon you to know what motivates him, what is his most destructive tool, and what is the nature of his poison by which he destroys men's minds and hearts. You shall soon behold some future events in which many things won't make any sense to you. Don't worry about what you don't understand. Just receive what you can." Paul sat down, holding Gabriel's hand and not letting go; for the darkness falling on them was horrifying. It was tangible and heavy, like the humid air in the midst of a long, August heat wave.

Paul looked down upon Lucifer, now Satan. He was seated at the head of a long conference table where all shapes and sizes of evil demons were sitting. Satan's face looked somewhat like an elderly beauty queen or retired TV star. You could tell that at one time, in the very distant past, he had been majestically handsome. But the long centuries of hating, cursing, and murdering had etched deep, sin-filled wrinkles upon his countenance.

The darkness in the room was so thick it could be

sliced. Dreariness, doom, and evil permeated the very atmosphere. Everyone appeared annoyed, distressed, and frustrated. All of them, except for Lucifer (as he was still called by his own) were dressed in army officer uniforms. He alone had the massive body of a fierce, intimidating dragon, with the face and torso of an evil angel. This was an exclusive meeting of the elite of his army. Only his five star generals were invited to this one. These were the highest-ranking principalities and powers of evil, rulers over nations, kingdoms, and regions of darkness.

The year on Earth was 1948 and Israel had just been declared a nation, after centuries of being dispersed throughout the world. Satan knew this marked the beginning of the latter days, the very last of the last days of man's existence on the fallen planet that had been his domain for centuries. He had a newspaper in his hand, which he threw down on the table with anger and hatred that even his closest comrades had never seen before.

"Why didn't you follow my orders, you idiots," he screamed at them all, leaning on his clenched fists. "I strictly demanded that you were not, under any circumstances, to allow those stinking Jews to go back to their land." His knuckles became white and his face twitched in fierce frustration.

One of the largest generals who was seated in the back started shaking hysterically with violent fear. His assigned principality was the Middle East. "Does that mean our time of torment is about to begin?" he screamed out. "Oh my Satan! Oh my Satan! What are we gonna do?"

"Shut up, you defeated coward!" Satan screamed at him.

"I can't stand it," he yelled. "I can't stand thinking about our future! "Especially with you, Lucifer telling me that . . . "

"Shut up, I said! Shut up." Satan quickly jumped on top of the table, shrieking like a bat so loudly that it drowned out the whining general's revealing words. As he flew over to the distraught general, he swung his massive tail at him. His stinger had by this time fully grown back and it dug into the side of the distraught demon's head. The general fell down in intense pain, writhing like an injured snake. Satan swooped down and ripped off the stars and medals from his uniform, and then proceeded to unmercifully stomp on him, like an elephant would squash an egg. All the other generals pretended not to watch Satan as he kept pounding his massive feet up and down on the tormented demon. No one realized that Satan wasn't so angry at the wretched being as he was with God.

After a long time Satan became bored with his violent crushing of this unfortunate general. He scooped up the remains of the groaning, barely breathing demon and tossed him as far away as he possibly could. Never again would that demon be able to speak, he was so lacerated and injured. Satan walked back to his seat, breathing out fire and anger. "I'll have no cowards in my army," he yelled out at the nervous occupants of the conference room. The intensity of his great wrath surfaced because he knew his kingdom of darkness was surely coming to an end. Israel's national rebirth pointed to the prophecies, the dreadful words predicting the fact that his years were truly numbered. But he wouldn't allow his army to know this.

No one moved an inch, or said a word while the crushing was going on. They all knew better. They had seen this happen so many times before. But never had Satan so violently demolished one of his own. They all supposed it was because the general failed to block Israel from becoming a nation again. Actually, it was because Satan's wrath was intensifying because he knew he had but a short time left. **(Rev. 12:12)**

"We all know the Deceiving Tyrant came into being just like all of us," Satan began with his clever lies. He walked back to his chair, but remained standing as he spoke. He scanned everyone's eyes, trying to detect if there was anyone else who wasn't believing what he was saying. "As I have told you in times past, the Tyrant was once merely an angel, like you and I. He just arrived a little sooner on the scene than any of us. But I was there when he first took the Throne. I remember confronting Him, asking, 'What are you doing?' He smirked and then whispered into my ears, 'I am going to convince the world that I always was; so I can be the God. I will be able to rule the world the way *I* want it to be ruled.' But his judgments will not stand," Satan bellowed as He raised his fists in defiance of *the* God. "For instance," he continued, "I was confined to the pit, was I not? And I escaped. I made a way of escape for all of us. And, yes, I know the Tyrant's Scriptures say that we will be eternally cast into a fiery lake one day. But don't worry. I'll be able to find a way to escape from there, also. There's no way that hell fire will actually be eternal. Just ask the liberal theologians. It doesn't make sense, so it therefore cannot be true. But I AM perfect in wisdom, and I have already figured out how to escape the jailhouse that awaits us. And I shall eventually destroy that egotistical, arrogant, overgrown angel!"

"Yes!" General Mammon proudly agreed.

"We will all help you," General Lust added, "and we will then share the glory with you!"

"That's right!" the generals screamed as they jumped to their feet and gave their leader a standing ovation. Some of them went overboard with their exuberance over the little speech, nearly exposing what they were desperately trying to hide from everyone, especially Satan—they were not completely convinced that he was telling them the truth. They weren't even sure if Satan was capable of telling the unadulterated truth about anything.

All the generals then flew away to their respective posts and assignments, all except for one of them whom Satan asked to stay around afterwards. Bee-elzebub wondered what he had done to be honored with the privilege of spending time alone with his leader; a rare occasion for even those closest to him.

"Oh, great General of generals! What a wonderful cursing it is for me to spend some private time with you!"

"Oh, shut up with that hogwash," Satan blurted out as he fell back down in his chair and put his head in his hands. "I have such a headache!" he moaned.

"A headache!" the general replied with astonishment. "I never knew you suffer from headaches, Mighty One!" Bee-elzeebub paused and looked down at his shaking legs. He was nervous, fearful, and at a loss as to what to say next.

"Well, I do get headaches," Satan snapped. "I go through more misery than you could ever imagine. You see, Bee-elzeebub, I'm in torment, and it's becoming unbearable. I've just got to have someone to tell my secrets to; someone to share with."

"But, Mighty Lucifer," the general objected, "you just shared your heart with all of us. And what a wonderful speech it was! How it gave us hope to carry on in our fight against the Tyrant's earthly creation."

Satan lifted up his head and flatly declared, "It was all a bunch of lies. Are you so dense? Can't you see that the only truthful thing that was said came out of the mouth of the general who went berserk?" He grabbed the paper on the table in front of him and tore it in half. "Israel is now a nation. Everything is happening just as the Tyrant has predicted, no matter how hard I try to stop Him. It's only a matter of time, and then I will be cast into a lake of everlasting fire."

Bee-elzeebub was stunned. True to his ingrained habitual deception, he said, "But you'll be able to escape. I'm sure you'll find a way of escape for all of us." He began to imagine how Satan would take over at the last minute and save the whole hellish host.

Satan was really letting his hair down. He knew

the general would not be able to handle the truth without losing his mind, just as the last ten generals he confided in had gone insane in their next conference meeting. But he didn't care. It gave him a few moments of relief, knowing that someone else shared his torment. It also greatly amused him to watch the cold, hard, irreversible facts crush the general's mind, as it had done to the others before him, flattening them with the force of an unstoppable tank.

"I will not be able to escape," the Devil replied. "Never. None of us will ever be able to escape the eternal lake of fire. It is God's holy, righteous, eternal judgment against sin, and it shall burn us forever. God has declared it, and it shall be fulfilled. No one can reverse it. Everything He says shall come to pass, exactly as He says."

Bee-elzeebub figured Satan was lying, as usual, and frantically tried to figure out the puzzle. "But, all of us, with our combined strength and wisdom will surely find a way of escape."

"Can fallen angels fight against Omnipotence, and win?" Satan snarled.

"What? Omnipotence? You mean . . . you mean, the Tyrant . . . *is* God! Are you telling me that He is the eternal, Almighty God?"

Satan slowly nodded his head.

"You mean . . . you've been lying to us, all these long centuries? Lying about seeing the Tyrant right after he came into existence, going up to the Throne?"

"I'm a good liar, aren't I?" Satan boasted with

heartfelt arrogance.

"Oh, my Satan!" the terrified fallen angel screamed. "We *are* damned! And there's not a doomed thing we can do about it! How could I have been such a fool to listen to you," he growled at his superior, whom up to this point had received only his admiration and respect. The anger and frustration then turned inward. "How could I have been so stupid," he lamented, hitting his head with his claws. Much to the delight and amusement of Satan, the distraught demon then banged his head on the thick table in immense frustration. After a few long minutes Bee-elzeebub lifted up his sore, swollen head and asked, "So, why are you spending so much time and energy in pumping us up with promises of glory? Why? Why are you telling us we will be promoted in proportion to the number of humans we're responsible for dragging into hell? Why go through all the aggravation if you know it's all in vain?"

"Because I hate Him!" Satan yelled as he raised his fists in defiance of the Holy One. The scream was so incredibly loud it pierced the general's ears with stabbing pain. "I detest Him with every fiber of my being," he screamed, getting louder and louder as he went. "If I could, I would kill Him! I'd slit his throat; I'd bash His brains in; I'd trample Him under my feet! I hate Him with a passion! Hatred has consumed every fiber of my damned soul and spirit! I despise Him and His Son and His Spirit!" He stopped to catch his breath, having exhausted every bit of strength as he poured forth his screaming declarations. "Since I can't get to them," he slowly continued, twisting the newspaper in his tense hands, "I'll use every ounce of my supernatural energy to drag as many of His created humans to hell with me. They are *His* creation. Destroying *them* is as close to destroying God as I'll ever get. I know there's no redemption ever available for any of us. We went beyond the point of no return a long, long time ago. The eternal lake of fire is our portion, and I know it. If I dwell on it too much the torment becomes unbearable. The only consolation I have is in knowing I'm causing pain to the Tyrant's heart by deceiving Adam's children into following my ways, and thus sharing my fate."

"So, do you know what I do, Bee-elzeebub?" Satan continued. I flood the minds of those earth dirtballs with pride. Pride will keep them from coming to the Christ. Arrogance will keep them from forgiving each other. But more importantly, haughtiness will keep them from asking God for forgiveness, and thus bar them from their heavenly homes. Those sick humans are so disgustingly proud," Satan said with glee, rubbing his hands with conceit over how well his plans are working. "They take pride in their nationalities, their culture, their talents, and their skills. Everything God blesses them with they take pride in. They are so proud about their puny spiritual accomplishment and their tiny resemblance to their Maker. Even those who follow the Messiah diligently are so easily filled with pride over how much they think they are like Him. He has everything to be proud about, and yet He's meek and lowly. The dirtball earthlings have so little to be truly proud about and they are so void of genuine humility. You should see all the Christians who take pride in how much they think they are like their God! How deceived they are," Satan laughed. He laughed so hard at the irony of this that he fell over on his back.

He was still lightly chuckling when he pulled himself together and rose to his feet. The other demon wasn't laughing. He was staggering like a boar with a spear piercing right through its chest. He was also shaking like a leaf; a leaf on the verge of falling into the air and down to the hard, autumn ground.

"If you whisper a word of this to anyone, I will crush you into tiny pieces! You understand?"

"Yeah, right," the demon angrily and sarcastically snapped as he rose to leave, furious at having been so cleverly lied to for so long. Realizing he had become dangerously disrespectful, he jumped into the air, frantically flapping his wings in an attempt to escape as fast as possible.

Satan grabbed his tail and with a powerful yank threw him down upon the conference table. The impact caused the table to split in two and cave in, with the general lying in the middle of it. The terrified demon crunched up in a ball, holding his arms over his head, wanting to shield himself from the blows soon to come from his cruel master.

Satan slowly walked over to the demon general and knelt down right next to his terrified face.

"Just think," Satan whispered with a sarcastic tone of pretentious sympathy, "if you had chosen to not follow me, you'd be in heaven right now, enjoying the marvelous presence of the Almighty God. Actually, He's not a cruel tyrant, at all. I AM!"

That was the straw that broke the camel's back. The demon's mental torment reached the lake-of-fire level—totally unbearable. He started screaming in anguish and he has never stopped. And he never will.

SEVEN
THE ABOMINATION
THAT CAUSES DESOLATION

Paul then looked down upon a vastly different scene that conveyed many things strangely unfamiliar to him. These were glimpses from the Book of Revelation, which he had never read because it had not yet been written. A beast rising out of the sea of humanity with seven heads and ten horns. Another beast rising with the horns of a ram, but who spoke like a lamb. The nations had been begging for a Messiah, a World Ruler, a Political Savior to come on the scene and bring peace to the chaotic world. This was the answer to their humanistic desires. Paul saw Satan seated upon a throne a few hundred feet above one of the major cities in Europe. Gathered around this Throne were twenty-four demon elders, with golden crowns on their heads. "King Nomed of the European Confederacy is soon to unite the earth under one flag, the United States of the World," the Devil began, speaking to his twenty-four bored elders. "I shall soon totally possess his body and soul and through him I shall reign over all people, nations, and tongues," he said, trying to sound interesting.

"Long live King Lucifer! May your kingdom last forever!" The twenty-four rulers chanted as they routinely fell on their faces and cast their crowns at their Master's feet, which were scaly, black, and scabby with long, unsightly toenails.

"Quit all that junk," Satan demanded. He jumped

off his tinsel throne and grabbed the nearest elder, angrily yelling, "Get up on your feet! There's no more time to play our stupid God games!" He ran to the next one and yanked him up also. He turned to another prostrated demon and impatiently kicked him in the face. "Get up! Everybody get up," he cried. "Listen, the Scriptures declare that we have just a few short years left before the Messiah arrives to begin His Millennial reign. All of you have been around long enough to know that every declaration from the Tyrant's mouth shall be fulfilled in its season. And the season of fulfillment is upon us."

"I'm not going to play around any more. We all know the lake of fire is our destiny. There's nothing that can be done to reverse that. So let's not waste any more precious time. Forget all the silly pretending that I'm God and that you are my servants. We are all self-damned rebels against the Most High God and we shall soon enter into our justly deserved, eternal punishment. But until we do, let's concentrate all our combined effort, strength, and wisdom upon one single goal."

"And what goal is that, Master?"

"To steal, kill, and destroy! Crush! Annihilate! Drag as many souls to hell with us as we possibly can, in the least amount of time. Look at Nomed down there," Satan said as he pointed down to the huge inaugural procession going on beneath them. "He's about to be sworn in as ruler of the world. As I possess him I shall give him my agenda. I need everyone's help in figuring out how we can use him to destroy as many people as possible, as quickly as possible."

"Well, Lucifer, this certainly is a change," one of the elders said, as they all relaxed and gladly put a stop to their silly, play-acting. Another elder then observantly remarked, "You've always been too proud to ask advice from any of us *inferior* beings before."

"I don't care about my pride or my reputation any longer," Satan snarled, being consumed with hatred and impatience. "Don't you understand? We're about to be cast into eternal fire. Who cares about what anyone thinks. I'm not interested in impressing you. I'm not concerned any longer about receiving empty worship from you creeps, or from anyone. All that's left inside my heart is hatred. I hate Him with my whole heart and soul. I wish I could destroy Him. But I have to settle with destroying His prized creation: humans. So let's all put our heads together and figure out what kind of plan to put in the heart of Nomed. We want the largest amount of people as possible to be damned along with us. There are literally hundreds of millions on the Earth right now whose destinies are in the balance."

Bee-elzeebub raised his hand and then spoke out, not waiting to be called upon. "There's about five hundred nuclear bombs in the Middle East alone. Let's instigate another world war, and we will blow the entire planet into a million, little pieces," he said with unspeakable joy.

"No, no, no! That won't work," Satan hastily replied as he walked back and forth in front of his counselors, cracking his knuckles and biting his nails. "No. The Tyrant has tons of angels around that area who would never permit anything like that to happen."

"Let's spread the famine that's in Northern Africa throughout the continent of Europe," another general said. "That should wipe out about a fifth of the world within, say, a year or two."

"Too risky," Satan mused. "If they die slowly they'll have too much time to turn their hearts to God at the last minute, like that stupid thief on the cross."

"Well, Lucifer, you're not giving us many options. If the Tyrant will not allow us to bomb the world to pieces, and if it's too risky to kill them in other ways, what choices do we have left?"

"Come on, leaders, think. Think of something new, something different. You have all been destroying people for thousands of years, now. Surely, together we can come up with some kind of scheme to massively destroy the multitudes. But it's going to have to be creative; you know, something original."

"Then we'll have to use the Tyrant's textbook if we're going to have any chance of becoming *creative*," a principality said rather sarcastically as he darted down to earth to snatch an old Bible from a deserted church building.

"Give me that book," Satan snarled as the general quickly came flying back into the tension-filled meeting.

"Did you have a passage in mind to read?" the offended demon said with sarcastic anger.

"Well, yeah," he said as he thumbed through the pages. He turned towards the back and tried to crack open the Book of Revelation. Volts of heavenly electricity

106

burst through the pages and knocked him to the ground. "It's not fair," Satan whined. "That happens every time I try to read that last book. God just won't allow me to read it."

One of the other principalities walked over to the glistening book and bravely picked it up. As he thumbed through the Old Testament he said, "If the Tyrant's authority is going to hinder our power from mass destroying Adam's offspring, then we'll just have to let Him do the destroying."

"Hummm," Satan replied, scratching his chin, as he stood up on his feet.

"What in Hades are you referring to?" someone else asked.

"Do you remember long ago when we stirred up our friend Balak, the King of Moab?"

"Yeah!" someone exclaimed, suddenly realizing where the principality was headed.

"Remember what happened when he hired Balaam, the compromising prophet to curse the people of God as they were in the wilderness en route to the Promised Land? What happened? They were uncursable. And they were invincible, too. Balaam could not curse what God had blessed no matter how hard he tried." **(Numbers 23:20)**

"That's right," Satan interjected enthusiastically, joining in on the conversation. "And then I showed Balaam the only way for Balak to have a chance at winning was to get Israel to fall into idolatry. Under my wise guidance the luscious-looking women of Moab came out to their camp to give the sojourners some raisin cakes and barley loaves. How sweet of them," Satan laughed.

"Yeah!" another principality interjected. "And these sweet women were dressed so sensual that the men of Israel kindly offered to walk them back home that evening."

"Much to the dismay of their wives," someone else chuckled.

"It was definitely one of my greatest victories," Satan continued, clearly remembering the details of that Old Testament tragedy. "On their way back to the Moabite towns, the women informed the men of Israel that they were very religious. The only way they ever had sex with strangers was if they would swear by their god that they would afterwards join them in their Moabite idol worship. What a crowd they had the following morning! Never before had Balak's idol temple been so packed. Never before had God been so angered, except when His people worshipped that dumb golden calf. But this time, not even Moses' intercession could stop God's wrath from falling. I just sat back and watched as God Himself rose up and judged the lustful adulterers. God Himself wiped out thousands in one day because of their sins."

"It wasn't just the sexual immorality, but the idolatry which caused such severe judgment to fall," someone correctly added.

"That's it," Satan said. "Idolatry! That's the weapon we will use. It carries with it its own built-in judgment. For it is written, *'All who worship deaf and dumb idols become like them.'* **(Psalm 135:18)** Yes, it is also written, *'A deceived heart is their portion.'* **(Isaiah 44:17-20)** Idolatry always calls down the judgment of spiritual blindness and deception on its participants."

He looked down on the scene below, with all the pomp and ceremony fit for a king. "Our president will declare that he is the Christ, that he is divine; that he is God. He will be worshipped, and the worship will call down God's wrath and destroy multitudes! Yes!"

"But Lucifer," someone objected, "how will this destroy the people? There have been many world leaders in the past who have gained the worship and adoration of their subjects without causing spiritual destruction."

"Yes, I know," he said. "But this will be different. Once our European Empire President gains worldwide spiritual acclaim through miracles, signs, and wonders, then I will pull out my masterpiece. Would you like to see my new plan ahead of time?" Satan said with the excitement of a talented juvenile delinquent.

Everyone eagerly shook their heads.

"Okay. Stand back," he said. He then snapped his fingers and whipped his arms into the air. A burst of smoke appeared and then as it cleared away, a statue of President Nomed appeared before them. It was a perfect, life-size, granite replica of the most powerful man in the world, the one in charge of a host of nations. "I will place thousand of statues just like this all around the world, in every major town," Satan said proudly.

All of the principalities gathered in front of it and looked into the statue's face. "It certainly looks like him," someone remarked.

"Look!" another one said. "Look, he's crying!" Sure enough, tears were beginning to miraculously stream down his granite face.

"Look at his lips," someone else exclaimed. "They're moving!"

"This is great," a general in the back said. "This miracle will surely grab the worship of many."

"Keep looking," Satan said with the pride of an over-rated, under-achieving artist. The eyes blinked and suddenly the mouth began to open! Then the granite statue spoke; authoritatively, miraculously, demonically: "Whoever does not worship President Nomed and his miraculous statues must be put to death. Blessed are they who worship him and his images . . . for he is God!"

"That's perfect!" they all enthusiastically agreed.

Satan proudly continued. "The talking image of the president will capture almost everyone's heart. Whoever worships it will immediately be judged with a loss of all spiritual discernment. That, in turn, will seal their eternal doom. It will therefore cause total spiritual destruction and desolation to its worshipers. That's one of the main reasons why God sees idolatry as such an abomination, you know. We will set these statues up everywhere; in parks, in malls, in McDonald's, even in the rebuilt temple in Jerusalem. It will be known in heaven as the abominable idolatry that caused total desolation, that is, the abomination of desolation. It will be known in hell as my final masterpiece!" Satan triumphantly exclaimed.

"I still remember the day King Nomed prayed to me," he continued, thinking out loud. "I have it down on record. He prayed, 'Oh, dear Lucifer, if you will give me the kingdoms of the world, I will give you my heart, body, and soul, forever.' I took him up on that offer. I've done my part. Now it's time for him to pay up. It's time for me to possess him. He's about to become much more than just demon-possessed, much more than just having legions of demons. Ready or not, he's about to become Satan-possessed. It's time for me to go. I've got to get those images set up as soon as possible."

Satan flew down towards the cheering crowds at the inaugural ceremonies of the Anti-Christ, the world ruler, the beast who speaks like a lamb, whose talking images will seal the doom of multitudes.

EIGHT
THE DESTINY OF EVIL

One thousand and three years later. Michael once again wrapped heavy chains around the devil and dragged him to the very edge of the lake that was filled with everlasting fire. "There will be no end to your torment now, Satan," Michael said with a mixture of sadness and indignation. "You will never, ever escape the horrible place in which you will soon be cast. Any last words?" Michael asked.

"Yes," Satan remarked as he fell to his knees. "Jesus Christ is Lord, and I AM . . . I AM AN UTTER FOOL!"

With those being the last words he ever spoke, Michael grabbed one end of the chain that was wrapped around Satan's reptilian body. He swung Satan around in a large, slow circle over his head, and then around again, and again and again, picking up speed with each rotation. Then he let go of the chain. The serpent sailed through the air and was cast into the lake of fire and brimstone. He screamed out, "NOOOOOO," as his body traveled for nearly half a mile.

Satan hit the lake with a bang. Upon impact, the molten lava splashed up like thickened soup. The fiery liquid then showered down upon his head, scorching his eyes and ears, but not fully consuming them. The lava burned away his chains, his wings, his arms, and his feet. All that was left was his torso and his head. He was left in the very same condition the innocent cherub was in after he had ruthlessly attacked it, many long centuries ago. The state of his first victim in his long career of cruel violence would forever dictate his eternal condition. Justice had finally caught up with him.

Satan frantically tried to stay above water, that is, above fire. But without any limbs, it was an impossible, lost cause. He soon succumbed to the inevitable and sunk down into the lake and drowned. He didn't die, however; that being an impossibility for an eternal being such as he. The tormented creature began to sink towards the bottom of the lake with the liquid fire covering his head and flooding into his mouth and lungs. The burning fire roasted his insides and caused incomprehensible pain. He soon touched the bottom of the lake, only to find it was covered with pointed spikes of brimstone, which pierced his torso and caused him to shriek out in agony and shake in spasms of pain.

"I now understand how sinful my rebellion against God really was," Satan thought to himself. "I now fully realize how unholy and horrible my acts of violence and iniquity have been in the sight of the Holy One." He didn't want to think these thoughts, strongly trying to prevent them from rising up into his tormented mind. To his dismay, the fires of hell were burning away the lies he had been spreading for so long that he had come to believe in himself. "I know the Holy One is righteous in all His ways and just in all His judgments. Since this eternal fire is the sentence He has seen fit to inflict upon me, my crimes surely were wicked to infinite proportions."

"No! The Tyrant is unfair," he screamed at himself,

arguing with the truth that was dawning upon his scorched soul. "No. I don't deserve this! I didn't know what I was doing. I wasn't aware of the consequences. No one warned me." He suddenly remembered all the long walks God the Father took him on, patiently, lovingly pleading with him to make the right choices while he was still an angel in heaven. With no one around to tempt, and no one to focus on destroying, Satan had nothing to place his mind upon and escape into, nowhere to run away from these truth-filled memories. The pure truths of the recollections were tormenting his mind, and there was nothing he could do to stop them from coming. The naked truth tormented his soul more than the outward fire and the piercingly sharp spikes on the bottom of this eternal lake. "It's true, it's true, it's undeniably true! God is righteous, and I am guilty. I deserve the punishment that is now my lot for eternity."

"No, no, nooooo," his soul screamed in protest to the thoughts of actuality. "I am righteous. I am God. I am the ruler of all. I have done nothing wrong, and I don't deserve to be here." He tried desperately to fight off the invading memories that were filling his mind and soul.

"Oh, please, please, Almighty God! Please, let me keep my refuge of lies. Don't let the full truth dawn upon my soul. I can't endure it! I can't!"

The currents in the lake swept through the area Satan was in and began to thrust him upward toward the surface of the lake. "Is God answering my prayer? No, this cannot be!"

His mutilated, scorched body somehow floated

back to the top. There were masses of other damned souls floating on the thick surface of the lake. They looked like a school of dead, rotting, fish in a polluted reservoir in some God-forsaken land. Some of them still had their limbs, but most couldn't move at all, being at the mercy of the current in a place where mercy had been forfeited, forever. All of them were completely conscious, regardless of the degree of their mutilation. Satan blinked his eyes, trying to remove the burning lava from them so he could focus in on the expanse over his head.

"There he is!" Gabriel declared.

Satan looked up towards his left and saw an angel and a human standing on a balcony at the edge of Paradise. They were looking out upon the corpses of those who had sinned against God. Gabriel recognized Satan and pointed him out to Paul.

"Is this the one **who made the earth to tremble, that did shake kingdoms?"** **(Isaiah 14:16)** Paul asked with utter amazement. "Him?" he asked again with his mouth wide open in disbelief, as he looked down upon the helpless, fallen angel. "He's the one who made the cities of the earth wastelands, and the one who bound the prisoners in chains?"

"Yes," Gabriel answered. "He's the one. Lucifer, Satan, the Accuser of the Brethren, that old Serpent, the Devil."

Satan tried to open his mouth to curse them, but was unable to since his vocal cords had been burned out and destroyed by the drowning fire. He was forced to listen to their conversation and to hear Paul describing

Satan's crimes: *"The one who made the cities thereof spiritual wastelands; the one who bound the prisoners into cruel and relentless chains of wickedness."* **(Isaiah 14:16-17)**

The fiery lake's horrible volcanic waves began spilling over Satan's sizzling, pain-filled head. He sank down and down and down, knowing the brimstone spikes were about to pierce through his torso once again, and again, and again, forever and ever, with no end, no rest, no mercy . . . ever.

"You know," Paul said thoughtfully and soberly, "the Book of Isaiah has always been my favorite prophetic book. I've read it so many times since I was a child that I've just about memorized the whole thing. I've carefully examined the last words penned through Isaiah's hand. I've meditated on them so very often. *'They shall go forth and look upon the corpses of the men who have transgressed against Me. For their worm does not die, and their fire is not quenched. They shall be an abhorrence to all flesh.'* **(Isaiah 66:24)** Now that I actually see what God was referring to, I realize how inaccurate my perception of the horror of eternal separation from Christ really was. Just look at all these tormented, lost souls," Paul groaned.

A sea of molten lava stretched as far as his eyes could reach, with hundreds of thousands of erupting volcanoes just below the surface. The lava ocean rose and fell in wave after wave of eternal torment. Everywhere, people and fallen angels could be seen helplessly drowning in the fiery brimstone. Some struggled immensely to stay afloat. These were mostly the newcomers to this horrible lake of fire. The others, along with Satan and his demons allowed the raging currents to carry them wherever it took them. The volcanic sea shook from the multiple massive eruptions taking place. All across the molten sea people and angels were dying, and yet never dying, and yet . . . continually dying.

"An everlasting garbage dump," Paul realized. All the inhabitants of this land were forever stripped of their many God-given talents, virtues, and gifts that had been bestowed upon them, given to them out of the sheer generosity and goodness of God, given to drive them to repentance. Now, all was taken away because of their stubborn unwillingness to turn away from their many sins. Everyone was also stripped of their refuge of lies. The atheists now believed; the idolaters had no idols to hide behind; the criminals had no cloak of darkness; the liars had no one to deceive. All deception was exposed and burned away.

Paul could hear the cries and shrieks, moans and groans, of the eternally lost, the eternally damned. They screamed as though they couldn't stand the suffering any longer, because they couldn't. But they had no choice, no other option available to them. During their time of decision-making, they neglected or refused to come to Christ. Like one million people in a crowded mental ward deprived of their suppressive medication their horror-filled screams permeated the air. Due to the pressures bearing down upon their poor, feeble lives, little by little, they were all losing their souls in the same way people on earth sometimes lose their minds. Their souls were collapsing under the weight of eternal punishment. As a caterpillar crossing a busy highway would have no chance to resist the oncoming tires of a truck, so these damned souls had not a chance to bear up under such punishment. They all sank down into eternal despair.

Paul noticed that not a single damned being was protesting against God; no one was accusing Him of any wrongdoing or unfairness. For they had all stood in front of the Great White Throne during their time of judgment and sentencing before arriving at their awful destination. The greatness of the brightness of that holy Throne overwhelmingly convinced all the ungodly sinners of the depths of their ungodliness. **(Jude 15)** They had sinned against infinite holiness, truth, and love. They knew infinite punishment was their just reward. The lost souls weren't even screaming at Satan and his demons who all shared in the same lot of forever drinking the wine of the wrath of Almighty God, poured out without mixture or dilution. **(Rev. 14:10)** All knew in their heart of hearts that Satan could not have chosen for them. He may have handed them the gun, but each one pulled the trigger by choosing to remain in the darkness of sin. They couldn't blame God at all. They each knew He had sent His only begotten Son into the world to be their Savior. This was absolutely the most tormenting thing about being trapped in this lake of everlasting fire; it wasn't the fire, the brimstone spikes, the actual pain, nor their tormented consciences, but the piercing realization that they didn't have to go there. They could have chosen Christ, instead.

They could have been enjoying the blessings of heaven for all eternity. But now, it was too late. The door of opportunity had closed upon them forever, and they all knew it.

"Such a fool. Such a condemned fool I am," Paul heard one of the nearby carcasses scream out. "He was calling me. He was calling me and I ignored Him. I loved the evil things of the world; I loved my money; I loved my women and my sin . . . and I ran from Him . . . the only One who truly loved me, the only One who could have set me free! Such a fool I am! God is just. This is what I deserve. This is truly what I deserve," he acknowledged as a huge wave of lava washed over him and drowned him in perdition and destruction.

Paul fell to his knees as deep tears flowed down his trembling cheeks. "It's what I deserved, also," he said to himself, "before the grace of God intervened in my life."

"Yes," Gabriel said. "And before we leave, it would be helpful for you to see the depth of truth in that statement before your very eyes."

NINE
ONE LAST SCENE

"This will be the last scene we view," Gabriel stated as Paul looked up through weeping, grateful eyes.

The new scene transposed before them was now filled with refreshingly familiar sights: the Judean countryside, the city of Jerusalem, and the eastern gate with its massive arch. Two men, or so it seemed, were walking through these gates in the early morning sunshine. Immediately Paul recognized one of them as none other than Lucifer. His common clothing couldn't conceal his brilliantly beautiful, totally arrogant countenance. But who was the one he was conversing with? He didn't recognize who Lucifer's companion was. The unrecognized one stopped and looked into a shop window, admiring his own reflection and his pompous, religious attire.

"Certainly, you are the most handsome Pharisee in these parts," the evil angel whispered into his ear.

"I AM certainly the most dignified Pharisee in the land," the man echoed as he turned his body slightly, admiring his physique, clothing, and looks.

Satan then said, "And you certainly should be a higher rank than you are. I'm sure as you continue to round up the heretics, the high priest will promote you to an appropriate position for someone as wise as yourself."

"I AM destined for greatness. I will continue to show the High Priest how zealous I am for the law," he parroted the Luciferian thoughts again. His conscience tried to tell him he should be doing all for God's glory alone, but the thoughts of pride were slowly gaining more and more ground. They walked further down the street and turned into a small traveler's inn.

"How many in your party?" the bored innkeeper recited.

"Just myself," the man answered as he and the wicked spirit sat down together, with the man's back facing Paul and Gabriel.

Paul glanced over at Gabriel with a questioning look. Gabriel replied, "The man isn't aware that Lucifer is with him. He thinks he's alone."

"This is quite interesting," Paul said as he stared even more intensely at the scene unfolding before them.

As the man ate the bread in front of him, the wicked spirit continued to pour his vile thoughts into his unsuspecting mind. "You are the most important Pharisee in Israel. Your zeal alone will stamp out the sect that is threatening to poison the gullible and ignorant people in this region. If only everyone was as intelligent as you are. Then they wouldn't be duped by every religious charlatan that comes along."

"If only everyone was at least half as smart as I am," the proud Pharisee said to himself as he sipped his water, and then finished his meal, totally unaware that Satan was inspiring his thoughts.

Upon leaving the inn a commotion could be heard inside the city, in the vicinity of the temple area.

"Don't go over there!" Lucifer demanded. "It's just another one of those political uprisings taking place.

Barabbas and his men are trying to start something again. It wouldn't be proper for a dignitary such as you to be seen at such an event. It's best to leave the city now and come back tomorrow morning."

The man looked up into the sky and discerned by the sun's position that it was nearly noon. "I'm meeting with the High Priest today regarding what to do with those imprisoned heretics who refuse to recant. I really need to be there," he thought to himself.

"The climate in the city is dangerous," Lucifer whispered vehemently. "With the political unrest, it's possible you might get hurt. You can tell the High Priest tomorrow that you were unable to make it because of the turmoil in the city."

"I can tell the High Priest that I decided it was too dangerous to come today," the man decided as he briskly walked out of the city gate and down a hill leading to a shortcut to the road to Jericho. Lucifer wiped his sweating brow in relief and flew away, darting towards the commotion happening inside the Holy City. The man felt a little cowardly as he continued walking away, pondering his strange decision.

"Who *is* that man that Lucifer has been subtly communicating with?" Paul asked Gabriel.

"You don't recognize him? That's you, Saul of Tarsus. The dedicated, yet proud Pharisee whose ears were tuning in to the voice of Lucifer; whose brilliant mind grew accustomed to his thoughts; whose heart was beginning to harden with demonic and religious arrogance. You considered yourself a godly man; you weren't an adulterer, a cheat, or a liar. But even so, Lucifer was your unrecognized companion and your heart began to swell with his arrogant ways."

"Saul is heading down to Jericho," Gabriel continued as he looked out on the scene below. "He was afraid of getting hurt by a politically violent mob. But in actuality, Barabbas and his group of cutthroats had by this time abandoned their lofty political reform ideas and had degenerated into nothing more than common thieves. They are about to rob and kill the rich-looking Pharisee who was on his way to the protection he was seeking in Jericho."

"Yes, I remember now." Paul solemnly and humbly stated. "Yes, it's all true. Thank God I decided to go back into the city."

"You decided?" Gabriel said with amusement. "Watch what really happened."

From their vantage point they could see the entire scene. Saul was about to turn a corner, which would place him on the road to Jericho and right into the ambush. Suddenly, the sky behind him was filled with the radiance of an angel shining brightly with the countenance and grace of the One whose presence he had just come from. An angel of grace for sure. He hovered over the nearby hills, searching for his assigned target. When he spotted the proud Pharisee he swooped down upon the path behind him, taking on the appearance of a fellow Pharisee.

"Saul, Saul am I glad to see you," the angel stated, pretending to be out of breath as he caught up with him on the road. "Saul, there's a mob forming outside the

Temple."

"I know," he said. "I, uh . . . " He didn't know what to say next, not wanting to sound like he was cowardly running away. "I heard there was a lot of political unrest in the city today."

"Political unrest?" the disguised angel said. "No. It's a mob of the Sanhedrin and high-ranking Pharisees. They've finally sentenced one of those Christ-followers to death. It looks like they're about to stone him. You've got to come and witness this."

"Of course," Saul said. "Finally, the Sanhedrin is taking concrete steps to snuff out this horrible sect! Finally." He turned and began running back towards the city, gaining momentum with each step. The thought then occurred to him, "How in the world did that Pharisee know I was on the road to Jericho?" He stopped and looked behind him and no one was anywhere in sight. "How peculiar," he thought. He began running again with all his might, forgetting about the incident as he became consumed with the hopes of assisting in the much-needed execution.

When he came into the city, he could distinctly hear the mob as they dragged Stephen out of the gate that was nearest to the Temple area. Saul was ecstatic! He eagerly searched for and found the High Priest and asked if he could join in the proceedings. Since he was still much younger than most of the Pharisees, he was only allowed to hold the coats and robes of the leaders who would perform the execution. He looked around at all the proud, die-hard Pharisees who made up the ruling council of the great Sanhedrin. And then he saw him. A simple looking man, with modest looking clothing, was silently standing there in the middle of the crowd. There was a distinct look of majesty on his face, **like the face of an angel. (Acts 6:15)** Such peace, such tranquility, such humility! He was looking up into the sky, as though he were gazing right into the face of God Himself. **"Lord Jesus, receive my spirit,"** he loudly declared as the hurling rocks began to pelt his body. In the midst of the shower of angry rocks, the man quietly and humbly fell to his knees in prayer. "Lord," he said loud enough for all who were listening to hear, *"Lord, lay not this sin to their charge!"* And then he died. **(Acts 7:59-60)**

Saul felt sick. He felt like he had the wind knocked out of him. "How could that man have been so forgiving and loving," Saul thought to himself. "He actually prayed for his persecutors and from his heart. How can this be? How could he so clearly embody the essence and spirit of Jehovah? How could he be so wrong and yet be so right? Perhaps . . . perhaps we're the ones who are so bent on being right, that we've become completely wrong."

Saul dismissed those thoughts and nodded his head in consent as one by one the Pharisees made their way over to him to retrieve their robes and coats. Saul looked deep into the eyes of these arrogant, egotistical, self-righteous men. Many of them were spewing out ungodly curses at the dead man and the family he had just left behind. Saul had never heard so many Pharisees curse before. This also shook him. "Did we do this act out of zeal for Jehovah, or out of animal rage?" he thought to

126

himself. "If it was out of zeal for God's glory, then why are so many of my colleagues speaking words which the Torah teaches should never be spoken? The Torah says we are to be loving and forgiving . . . like . . . like that dead man over there was."

Compared to the faces of these unholy "holy men" who paraded past Saul, Stephen surely looked angelic. Saul walked toward the martyr and took another look at his face, which was still shining. Actually smiling, Saul observed.

Lucifer nervously walked over and whispered into his ear, "A condemned heretic!"

Saul's conscience spoke back in protest, "How could Stephen have been so wrong and his spirit so right? If people would stone me to death, would those be my gracious, last words? I don't think so."

"You see how subtle these deceivers are!" Lucifer yelled into his mind. "If this group isn't stamped out within the year, they will cover the entire nation with their heresies. The great Pharisaic traditions will be abandoned for this false cult and the nation will never be the same."

"No!" Saul yelled out so loud, many stopped and curiously looked his way. "No," he said a little softer, but with even more vengeance. "This cult will be wiped out by the end of the year, if it's the last thing I do." He picked up a rock and threw it at the nearby peaceful carcass. Although he was only a few yards away, his aim was way off because he was shaking with such anger. The smiling face of the dead disciple of Jesus the Nazarene seemed to be saying, "Do what you may, but you will never be able to stamp out of your mind the love, peace, and true humility you've witnessed in me today."

For the next few months, Saul channeled all his energy into persecuting the fledgling church. Lucifer spent most of his efforts on keeping his prized Pharisee too busy to ponder the thoughts his conscience wanted to dwell on. Saul, the inquisitor, went so far as to travel to distant cities to round up all the believers he could find, dragging them into prison, and compelling them to blaspheme their Savior. As hard as he tried, however, he was unable to remove from his memory the look on Stephen's face. "Do what you may, but you can't stamp out of your mind the love, peace, and humility you've seen." The images and the words continually came back to haunt his conscience. His mind would have nothing to do with them, but his conscience couldn't help but face the fact that Stephen was the godliest man he had ever seen.

Saul was riding towards Damascus one day, with permission from the High Priest to arrest all the ignorant followers of the Nazarene that were living there. As his horse and those with him swiftly sped to their destination, his mind wandered back to the day of the martyr's death. "The only man I've ever seen who even came close to displaying such genuine humility was my father. How I wish he were still alive. He would tell me what to do about these nagging recurring thoughts dealing with the possibility that Stephen might have been right, and I might have been wrong . . . terribly wrong. Oh, I wish my dear father was still alive!"

A scene from childhood flashed through his mind.

He and his dad were visiting his uncle on a farm in the countryside in the region of Galatia. The crisp autumn sky was filled with white, puffy clouds, inviting all creation to rejoice in their bountiful Creator. But there was no rejoicing on the farm that particular day.

"I don't understand it, Alex," his uncle anxiously said to Saul's dad. He's the best ox I have. He's strong; he's faithful. But even so, if he keeps kicking against the goads, he's going to cripple himself."

The uncle showed his brother (and his very curious young nephew) exactly what he was talking about. His two oxen were yoked together with a large harness. On their sides were placed steel rods that kept them from plowing crooked furrows. If either one moved too much out of line their legs would hit against the goads and cause sufficient pain to straighten them up.

"Just look at his swollen right leg," the uncle said with compassion and concern.

Saul's father went over to the ox's lowly face and caressed his nose, speaking in his strong, compassionate way: "I wish I could read your mind and find out how to stop you from destroying yourself. If you think you're going to win the battle with the goads, you're sadly mistaken. It's hard for you to kick against the goads, isn't it old fella?"

Saul's horse suddenly jostled over a small stream, waking him from his vivid memories. "I feel just like that ox," he said to himself. "It seems as though that dead man's countenance is like those steel goads. How can I reconcile the truth that he was such a godly man, but at the same time be so sure that he was part of an evil cult? Oh, God," he said from the very depths of his soul, "God of my ancestors, Abraham, Isaac, and Jacob, have mercy on my confused soul, and show me the truth."

At that precise moment, lightning struck. Saul was knocked off his horse onto the hard ground. He looked up and realized the bolt of lightning was a bolt of Light, brighter than the sun, hovering over him. This Light had the appearance of a person, the gentleness of his father, the humility of Stephen, and the majesty of what he always thought Jehovah God was like, to those who could somehow get close enough to capture a glimpse of Him.

"Saul, Saul, why are you persecuting Me?"

"Who are you, Lord?" the trembling Pharisee replied.

"I am Jesus of Nazareth, whom you are persecuting. It is hard for you to kick against the ox-goads." (Acts 9:4)

Suddenly the scales fell from his eyes and he realized that Jesus is the true Messiah. The loving rebuke pierced right into his heart. Saul threw off his pharisaic attitudes and allowed his heart to accept the undeniable facts.

"I have been like a dumb beast before Your holy face, dear Lord. Oh, please forgive me. I have been driven by my arrogant pride, blinded by my religious prejudices, and deluded by my traditions. But now I see. Now I see You! You're the One Daniel said would be **cut off for the transgressions of the people;** the One Moses declared would be **raised up among the brethren;** the

130

suffering servant Isaiah wrote about; the One who was **wounded for our transgression, bruised for our iniquities."** (**Daniel 9:26; Deuteronomy 18:15; Isaiah 53;5**) Scripture after scripture came flooding to his keen mind, as his vast intellect was now being utilized by the Holy Spirit to prove the reality of what his heart was experiencing, instead of denying what his conscience was hinting at for so long.

This Messiah was quite different than what Saul pictured Him to be. Instead of being majestically proud, He was magnificently humble. Instead of cold and exacting He was loving and compassionate. At the same time He was overflowing with pure truth and holiness.

Saul's heart bowed in deep reverence and awe to this great One who had broken through from heaven upon his tormented soul. "My Lord and my God, one glimpse of You, and You have captured my heart. I'm Yours, forever and ever. What would You have me to do?"

"Rise to your feet," the Divine Bolt of Light said. *"For this purpose have I appeared to you—to appoint you a witness both of these things which you see and of those things which I will appear unto you: delivering you from the people and from among the Gentiles, unto whom I am now sending you—to open their eyes, that they may turn from darkness to Light, and the power of Satan to God, that they may receive remission of sins, and an inheritance among them who have been made holy by faith in Me."* (Acts 26:16-18)

Tears of gratitude streamed down Paul's face as he watched his conversion taking place before his eyes. He then turned and asked Gabriel, "I wasn't disobedient to the heavenly vision, was I?"

"No, Paul, you sure weren't."

TEN
THE WISDOM GIVEN TO PAUL

The scenes before them dissolved away, indicating the end of the book-door. Gabriel stood on the edge of the balcony and stared out into the distance for quite a long while, remembering much more than what was portrayed to Paul. "It's been a while since I've seen the many events depicted in this book," Gabriel finally stated as Paul rose to his feet. The angel motioned with his hand toward the door behind them, and then followed Paul back into the library. He asked a very quiet, subdued Paul, "Did that minister to you?"

"Did it ever!" Paul exclaimed.

"Have you learned something about the enemy?" Gabriel inquired, knowing full well the answer to that question, but wanting to hear Paul say it.

"Oh, yes," Paul replied without hesitation. "Pure hatred is his motivation, idolatry is his most destructive tool, and pride is the poison in his nature by which he infects the nature of man and leads him on the pathway to hell. But you know, these truths about pride would have been so useful during my sojourn on Earth. They would have been even more helpful than understanding the origin of evil."

"That's the way of the kingdom," Gabriel replied. "Often, in our search for a particular truth, God will gently guide us into the discovery of things much more needful to us than what we were originally looking for. So often, people don't initially seek to understand what they really need to know. But the all-seeing Father knows what's best for us and He will lead and guide us into all truth; both the truths we desire to know and the truths we desperately need to know. You were drawn to this particular book because of your curiosity regarding the origin of evil. The story line went way beyond that subject into more helpful truths, didn't it? Besides, what you've learned about the beginning of evil probably has triggered even more questions than you ever had before you saw this book. So it is with many of the deep things of God. As Moses aptly said, *'The secret things belong to the Lord, but the things which are revealed belong to us and our children.'"* **(Deuteronomy 29:29)**

Paul nodded his head in total agreement as he took a deep breath and looked around the bright library, collecting his many thoughts. He turned and gazed upon the beautifully handsome, friendly angel standing next to him, deciding to completely confide in his new friend. "Gabriel, some of the scenes I've just witnessed have brought varying degrees of anguish into my soul. Is it possible for a glorified Christian to feel anguish in heaven? Am I yet in my glorified body, or is just my spirit here. Am I **in the body or out of the body? I cannot tell."** **(2 Corinthians 12:3)** Paul spoke with the utmost sincerity and seriousness, continuing before the angel could answer. "But even more pressing on my heart is this. I so wish that I had taught more about the dangers of pride to those under my care. How I wish God would have used my life to truly and solemnly warn others of its subtle poisons!"

"Regrets are not allowed here, in the kingdom of heaven," the angel said with an unusual smile on his holy face.

Paul wondered what he was hinting at, but just as he was about to ask, King Jesus walked through the front door of the heavenly library. He gave Paul a big, comforting hug and motioned for him to take a walk with Him outside. They walked down a heavenly road together for a while without either one speaking, simply enjoying each other's company.

The pathway led right up to a large, crystal stream. Paul immediately noticed there was no bridge in which to cross over, yet the pathway continued directly on the other side. "How do we cross over?" he asked his Lord. King Jesus, as magnificent as He is, couldn't help but let out a hearty laugh at Paul's concern. "This is the River of Life, Paul. We don't have to worry about crossing over it. We can walk through it!"

"But won't we drown?" he asked, not realizing how silly it was to think that a person in heaven could actually drown.

"No. We won't drown. Let's go together," Jesus said patiently and reassuringly as He put His arm around Paul's shoulder.

Paul was still shaken up by the scenes of hell he had just witnessed. For this reason Jesus took him by way of the crystal river. The water of life had a way of washing away pain and sorrow.

As Jesus and Paul ventured farther out into the river the water flowed through their beings, refreshing their souls as a warm shower invigorates the outward body on Earth. Jesus said to his dear friend, "As the water goes over our heads, you need not worry about holding your breath. Just open your mouth and drink in the water; as much as your heart desires."

Paul opened his mouth and followed his faithful Lord's instructions, drinking in the water of life. When they came to the other side, Paul noticed they weren't dripping wet, as he had supposed they would be. In this land of perfection, nothing could ever spoil, decay, or be out of place in any way, even for a moment.

"Thanks, Lord," Paul said. "I feel much, much better."

They climbed up a soft, green hill and sat down on a bench that seemed to be waiting just for them, waiting just for that moment. The King casually began to point out some of the various sights and people before them, taking great delight in the thrill it gave to Paul's redeemed soul. "Look over there," Jesus said, "That's Moses and Joshua. You'll get to meet them a little later. They're walking over to the open air amphitheater, where the greatest preachers of all time get to do what they love . . . preach about the glories of the Gospel of their salvation."

After what seemed like a long, wonderful afternoon of enjoying each other's company Jesus jumped to His feet with the excitement and agility of a child and then gave Paul a helping hand up.

"Let's go over there," Jesus said, leading Paul to an even larger hill from where they had a spectacular view of the distant holy city of God, the *New Jerusalem adorned like a bride for her groom.* (**Revelation 21:2**)   The faraway buildings sparkled with many varied gems and precious stones.   A fork in the road met them at the summit of the hill.   To the left was the path leading back to the gate Paul came through on his journey from Earth. To the right was the road to the city, the location of the throne of the Holy, Heavenly Father.

"Oh, I shall soon see the face of the Father!" Paul exclaimed with great, overwhelming excitement.   Jesus looked at Paul with eyes of love and compassion, a look that seemed to penetrate through and examine Paul's very soul.   His piercing glance reminded Paul of the things deep down inside, that were puzzling his spirit.   Paul knew that his Lord already was fully aware of what was troubling him.   "Jesus," Paul slowly began, "as much as the river and Your undivided attention have refreshed and restored my soul, I still have one little question in my heart. If heaven is a place with no burdens, then why am I so burdened to teach young Timothy some of the things I've learned?"

Jesus lovingly smiled and pointed to flashes of lightning that were rising up to heaven from the Earth.

"What are those lights?" Paul asked.   "Are they comets, or lightning, or . . . what are they, Lord?"

Jesus turned and faced him, affectionately putting his gentle but strong carpenter's hands on Paul's shoulders. The Lord looked into his eyes, sighed deeply and said, "Those lights are the fervent prayers of the disciples in Lystra who have surrounded your lifeless, earthly shell. They're asking Me to resurrect you, so you can continue to preach My Word a little while longer on Earth. They're praying according to My will, my beloved Paul. You are destined to write young Timothy of Lystra instructions, which will eventually teach many other people around the world."

Paul fell to his knees and said, "My gracious Redeemer and Lord, I choose with all my heart, again and again and again, to love and obey You and to do Your will, whatever the cost and wherever that will leads me to go. Your will is my command. My delight is to please You in all things."

He rose to his feet, hugged the Lord real hard and long and then they both walked out the gates of Paradise together and down a grassy hill. The hill got steeper and steeper as they went. Jesus was holding tightly onto his beloved Paul. When it got too steep to walk down any more the Lord lovingly asked, "Ready?"

Paul took a deep breath, closed his eyes and nodded his head. He felt no fear as he plunged into the mortal darkness below. He suddenly was back into his torn, battered, and bruised body. He had a hard time opening his eyes due to the amount of blood that had covered his face. He felt the hard ground beneath him and became aware of the sound of the fervent prayers of his beloved friends. Barnabas was leading the prayer with Timothy, Titus, and the others enthusiastically adding their "Amens," and "Yes, Lord, raise him up."

Paul summoned up as much strength as he could muster and then yelled out, "Amen!" It startled everyone! They just stared at him, being too shocked to move. Paul then raised his right hand, saying, "Barnabas, would you please help me up?"

Barnabas, along with everyone else, was still too shocked to move. Paul was alive! They couldn't believe it! It was too good to be true!

"Barnabas, Timothy, somebody . . . help me up!"

Suddenly they all reacted. Everyone now was helping him to his feet.

"Paul, you're alive! You're alive," they exclaimed with tears of excitement. One of them, who was filled with unbelief, nonchalantly whispered, "I guess he never actually died."

By this time Barnabas' handkerchief had sufficiently wiped enough blood off his face for Paul to see. He looked around in amazement and asked, "How long have you been praying?"

"About fifteen minutes," Timothy replied. "Why do you ask?"

"Oh, it seemed like I was in heaven for a long, long time."

"Tell us what you saw and what you learned."

"That would take a while," Paul replied. "It may even take years," he added with a heavenly smile, gazing up into the sky.

"Let's head back to our house, Paul," Barnabas interjected, ending the interrogation of the resurrected Apostle. "We don't want the officials to decide they need to stone you again in order to keep you down!"

"I think both of you should leave Lystra immediately and escape to Derbe for a while," Timothy said thoughtfully. "At least long enough for the antagonism against us dies down."

"It will never totally die down," Titus commented.

"That's true; but we should take up Timothy's suggestion," Barnabas conceded. "We'll get a good night's sleep and depart early in the morning for Derbe. We'll return in a few weeks. Let's get going."

As they hurried away, Paul grabbed Barnabas' arm and whispered into his ear, "Oh, by the way, I now realize you're right about the advice you gave me this morning regarding Timothy. Let's make sure we don't lift up a novice too soon, or he'd be in danger of falling into the same condemnation as the Devil."

Barnabas looked at Paul with intense curiosity, wondering how he was able to so quickly see eye to eye with him on a subject they sharply disagreed upon earlier that day.

The next day Paul departed with Barnabas to Derbe. And when they had preached the gospel there and made many disciples, they returned to Lystra, Iconium, and Antioch, strengthening the souls of the disciples, exhorting them to continue in the faith, and saying, "We must through many tribulations enter the kingdom of God." So when they had appointed elders in every church, and prayed with fasting, they commended them to the Lord in whom they had believed. (Acts 14:20-23)

Years later, while writing from a prison cell to Timothy, his son in the faith, he instructed him on the type of person to be selected as a pastor. *"A bishop then must be blameless, the husband of one wife, temperate, sober-minded, of good behavior, hospitable, able to teach . . . not a novice, lest being puffed up with pride he fall into the same condemnation as the devil."* (**1 Timothy 3:1-6**) Paul lived what he preached and became a model believer as the humility of Christ was formed deep within him. He could declare to the Ephesians, *"You know, from the first day that I came to Asia, in what manner I always lived among you, serving the Lord with all humility."* (**Acts 20:18-19**)

It's interesting to note that both Lucifer and Saul of Tarsus experienced a change of names to go with their inward transformations. Lucifer became Satan and Saul became Paul, the Apostle. Regardless of what Paul did or did not see while he was caught up into Paradise, it can truly be said that he experienced two miraculous conversions. His first conversion on the road to Damascus was surely a miracle, immediately changing him from Saul, the religious persecutor, to Paul the servant of Christ and His church. The second conversion transformed him from having a proud, pharisaical soul into becoming an extremely humble servant of the Lord. This type of conversion, which is never instantaneous, was what Jesus was referring to in **Matthew 18.** *"At that time the disciples came to Jesus, saying, 'Who then is greatest in the kingdom of heaven?' Then Jesus called a little child to Him, set him in the midst of them, and said, 'Assuredly, I say to you, unless you are converted and become as little children, you will by no means enter the kingdom of heaven. Therefore whoever humbles himself* *as this little child is the greatest in the kingdom of heaven.'"* If we come into an abundance of visions and revelations like Paul did, we must also hope for and ask God to also give us his revelation of the dangers of the original sin—pride.

In a book about the legacy of Lucifer one would think the two main characters would be the Devil and the Lord Jesus. I have deliberately chosen to have the Apostle Paul as the contrasting character to Satan. The reason is that, contrary to what Satan would have us to believe, Jesus Christ is in a completely different league than him. Satan is a finite, created being. The Lord is the Almighty, Eternal Son of God. No opposite and equal forces here! Also, over half of the New Testament focuses upon Paul's life. I believe this is for those of us who would have a tendency to say, "I can't live like Jesus. He's the holy Son of God." Often Paul said, under the inspiration of the Holy Spirit, *"Imitate me, just as I also imitate Christ."* (1 **Cor. 11:1; 4:12; Phil. 3;17, 4:9; 1 Thess. 1;6,7; 2 Thess. 3;7-9)**

In his last Epistle, written to Timothy, Paul boldly declared, **"Thou hast fully known my doctrine, manner of life, purpose, faith, longsuffering, charity, patience, persecutions, afflictions, which came to me at Antioch, at Iconium, at Lystra; what persecutions I endured: but out of them all the Lord delivered me. (3:10-11)** He went on to say, **"The time of my departure is at hand. I have fought a good fight, I have finished my course, I have kept the faith: Henceforth there is laid up for me a crown of righteousness, which the Lord, the** righteous judge, shall give me at that day: and not to me only, but unto all them also that love his appearing." (4:6-8)

Paul was martyred by the Roman Emperor Nero around 60 AD. His wisdom lives on through the letters he wrote which have been preserved for us in the New Testament.

CONCLUSION

Whenever someone takes a close look at the downfall of Lucifer, many truths come to light. First of all, to say that God created evil and sin is, in my opinion, like saying that God is the one who made the atom bomb. It is true to say that God the Creator made 1) all the various parts of the atom, 2) the latent power built within those atoms, and 3) the mental ability within man to one day figure out how to split the atom, and thus release its energy. God also gave man the ability to choose to use this knowledge to destroy many innocent people. But still God cannot be held responsible for the deaths caused by the bombs we have chosen to detonate upon our fellow humans.

In the same way, the making of the "bomb" of evil and sin in the universe lies at the feet of the Prince of Darkness, Satan. It is wrong to blame God over the occurrences of evil. Yes, He allowed wicked men to drop that horrible bomb on Hiroshima. Yes, He allowed people to do horrible things to other people. He has allowed angels to choose, and thus, He has allowed them to turn against Him. He allowed Adam and Eve to choose, and thus He also allowed them to fall into sin. Our infallible Bible, though, declares that God cannot sin. *"He is the Rock, His work is perfect; for all His ways are justice. A God of truth and without injustice; righteous and upright is He."* (Deuteronomy 32:4)

But couldn't God have prevented all evil from

coming into existence? Sure He could have. He can do anything. He could have prevented even the possibility of evil. But He didn't and He knows what's best, and it's impossible for Him to do wrong or even be tempted by evil. **(James 1:13)** I'm not sure what all the possibilities were when God was creating the universe. I'm glad that He didn't choose to make us mere robots, forcing us to always do what's right by not giving us an ability to choose.

But what would life be like if God had chosen to prevent even the possibility of evil? He *could have* made us no more than programmed computers. (I can imagine a cherub in heaven coming up to me in eternity and saying, 'I *choose* to forgive you for insinuating in your book that cherubim are not much more than robots.' I'm sure they are far more glorious than I could ever comprehend. I've grossly simplified them in the preceding story mainly because I know so little about them.) Angels and mankind could have been created without the ability to choose. (Since Adam's fall, however, we are not truly free to wholeheartedly and consistently choose righteousness until Jesus Christ graciously breaks the power of sin off of our lives. See **Romans 6**)

The only way, as far as I can see, that evil could have been avoided altogether was for God to never give any other created being enough freedom to actually choose anything substantial. God did not see fit to do this, and I, for one, am glad.

Through the words that Jesus spoke concerning Satan, we can understand something very important about him. Jesus clearly labeled Satan the father of lies. In John chapter **8**, Jesus said, **"Ye are of your father the devil, and the lusts of your father ye will do. He was a murderer from the beginning, and abode not in the truth, because there is no truth in him. When he speaketh a lie, he speaketh of his own: for he is a liar, and the father of it."** A father is someone who has children, as Abraham begat his son, Isaac. Satan gave birth to lies. Lying was birthed through his heart. Notice, however, that he wasn't named *a* father of lies, but rather *the* father of lies. Satan was the father of the first lie. I believe the Word show us that he is also *the* father of pride, *the* father of lust, and *the* father of sin. Through his downfall we see the origin of evil.

R.C. Sproul, the well-respected evangelical theologian, in his book, <u>Reason To Believe</u> has a chapter entitled, "If There Is A God Why Is There So Much Evil In The World?" He writes, *"If God is perfect, how can there be evil in the world? Beyond the question of suffering we must face the question of how we account for the presence of wickedness in the world. The question of the origin of evil has been called the "Achilles heel" of Christianity. This vulnerable point has been the subject of considerable philosophical speculation and criticism.*

The force of the question can be illustrated by the dilemma posed by many critics such as John Stuart Mill. The dilemma is frequently stated as follows:

If God desires there to be evil in the world, then He is not good. If He does not desire there to be evil, yet evil exists, then He is not omnipotent. Thus, if evil exists God is either not loving or not all-powerful. Evil casts a shadow over God's love and power. This is no small dilemma, and answers to it are exceedingly difficult."

After citing a few philosophical arguments, Brother Sproul concluded the chapter by stating, *"The question of the origin of evil has not been answered satisfactorily."*

This story about Lucifer originally came to me as I was facing situations that threatened to undermine my faith. (See Introductory Poem on page 3.) I was prayerfully meditated upon Satan's downfall, having spent almost a decade wrestling with how evil could come into existence without God creating it. Quite suddenly, the picture of Lucifer shutting the door on the Light flashed into my mind. Evil, or spiritual darkness, was birthed within the womb of Lucifer's willful choice of turning away from the Light. That picture, ingrained into my spirit, has been of more value to me than a thousand philosophical and theological words.

As I was finishing this story, I ran across a number of church leaders who seemed to see eye-to-eye with me on my conclusions. For example, in the book "Augustine on Evil," G.R. Evans writes, *"The condition of his mind seemed to him to have changed not metaphorically but literally from darkness to light. In a sentence he gives us the principle which solved for him the problem of evil: Where light shines there cannot be darkness. When light comes darkness proves to be simply the absence of light. Where there is good, evil is driven out; it proves to have been simply the absence of good. The notion was grasped in an instant . . . it was an idea for a surprising capacity for development. It enabled him to solve a great many of the problems, which had long troubled him. He spent the rest of his working life as a Christian writer exploring its implications."*

Evans also pointed out in the same book, *"Before he could make any headway with a solution to the problem of evil, Augustine had to shift his ground and see that the root of the trouble lay with man. If God had anything to do with evil, its presence in the world would be intolerable to the minds of his rational creatures, for it would make him either himself evil, or a weak and feeble God who could not resist evil. Only on the hypothesis that he gave his intelligent creatures so supreme a freedom that they could choose to turn away from him could God's good creation be seen to be capable of evil."*

William Gurnall in his puritan classic, The Christian In Complete Armour, writes, *"The birth of sin. Who is its father? The holy God disowns it. The sun can produce darkness sooner than the Father of lights can be the author of sin. God throws sin on the devil's doorstep to find its father . . . Satan conceived sin in the womb of his own free will."*

Jeffrey Burton Russell writes in The Prince of Darkness about the views of the famous leader of the early church named Tertullian who lived around 200 A.D. *"Tertullian helped form the Christian view that the reason God gave angels and humans freedom to sin was that a world without free will would be a world of mere puppets. God created the world in order to extend or expand the total sum of goodness, and goodness could be increased*

149

only by making creatures free to choose the good freely. God could not provide thus for good without allowing also for evil, since true free will entails the real possibility of choosing evil." Regarding Origen's (c. 185-254) beliefs he wrote, *"The Devil is the source of all evil, yet all things come from God. How can these statements be reconciled? God created the cosmos, said Origen, in order to add to the sum total of goodness. Since moral goodness requires freedom of choice, God created beings with true freedom. Without it the world would be incapable of good and therefore pointless. Such freedom entails the ability to do evil. God could not, so the argument goes, create a world in which real good exists without creating one in which real evil also exists. . . Satan's moral choice, Origen said, was to prefer nonbeing and purposelessness to real being and true purpose. The great angel who sung among the seraphim chose to debase himself."*

Matthew Henry, whose commentary on the Bible has been a favorite for centuries, wrote a comment regarding **Isaiah 45:7** where God declares, **"I form the light, and create darkness: I make peace, and create evil: I the Lord do all these things."** *"There is no God beside Jehovah. There is nothing done without him. He makes peace, put here for all good; and creates evil, not the evil of sin, but the evil of punishment.* (The New King James rightly translates it this way, **"I make peace and create calamity.***) He is the Author of all that is true, holy, good, or happy; and evil, error, and misery, came into the world by his permission, through the willful apostasy of His creatures, but are restrained and overruled to His*

150

righteous purpose. This doctrine is applied, for the comfort of those that earnestly longed, yet quietly waited, for the redemption of Israel. To contend with Him is as senseless as for clay to find fault with the potter. Let us turn God's promises into prayers, beseeching Him that salvation may abound among us, and let us rest assured that the Judge of all the earth will do right."

Yes, evil came into existence by God's permission, through the willful apostasy of His creatures, but even so, all evil is somewhat restrained, often overruled and always made to somehow fit into God's righteous plans for this world. Joseph echoed this truth to his brothers in **Genesis 50:20.** *"But as for you, you meant evil against me; but God meant it for good, in order to bring it about as it is this day, to save many people alive."*

For many of us, this explanation for the existence of unchecked evil seems unsatisfactory and incomplete. For those who have been deeply hurt by the evil choices of others, it just doesn't make sense why God allows such things. You might be inclined to ask, "Where was the Lord when so many Jews were suffering at Auschwitz, Germany?" To answer that I'd turn to one of my favorite verses from the Bible, though one that is not very well known. **Isaiah 63:9a says, "In all their affliction He was afflicted."** The Book of Judges echoes that truth where it says, **"His soul was grieved for the misery of Israel." (Judges 10:16b)** God was there in the affliction with them, grieving over their misery caused by the choices of evil men.

You may say, "That is not an intellectually

satisfying answer. It's an answer that speaks more to the heart than to the mind." Not that we are to disregard our mental abilities, but the truth is, there are certain things we will not be able to grasp until we enter into eternity. Only then will we have a full and complete perspective on every issue we now wrestle with. Moses said in **Deuteronomy 29:29**, *"The secret things belong unto the Lord our God: but those things which are revealed belong unto us and to our children for ever..."* We must come to God out of a response of what has been revealed to us: a sacrificial death for our sins on the Cross. As the song says, "It is enough that Jesus died, and that He died for me." That is all the proof we need that God is the fullest and most perfect source of love, and that He loves us deeper than we can imagine. So whatever the "perfect" explanation is for the existence of evil, it will reflect the perfect love of the One who laid down His life for us all.

Listen to the words that were anonymously inscribed on the walls of a cellar in Cologne, Germany, where several Jews were hiding from the Nazis: "I believe in the sun when it is not shining. I believe in love even when feeling it not. I believe in God even when He is silent." (Eliezer L. Erhmann, ed., Readings in Modern Jewish History: From the American Revolution to the Present) There are times when God is silent and there are times when He speaks loud and clear. Through the life and death of Christ, God the Father has spoken loudly, and clearly, His words of love and truth to us all. Hebrews 1:1-3 states, *"God, who at various times and in various ways spoke in time past to the fathers by the prophets, has in these last days spoken to us by His Son, whom He has appointed heir of all things, through whom also He made the worlds; who being the brightness of His glory and the express image of His person, and upholding all things by the word of His power, when He had by Himself purged our sins, sat down at the right hand of the Majesty on high..."*

Why do we even have to deal with this pit of evil that mankind has fallen into? Perhaps a more useful question would be, "How are we going to deal with the situation we find ourselves in?" John C. Maxwell, in his message entitled, "Lifting People To A Higher Level" has some needed insights. He said, *"Jesus all His life lifted people to a higher level. To show you the difference between Jesus and us, let me share with you one closing thought:*

A man fell into a pit and couldn't get himself out.

A subjective person came along and said, "I feel for you down there."

An objective person came along and said, "It's logical that someone would fall in that pit."

A Christian Scientist said, "You only think that you are in a pit."

A Pharisee said, "Only bad people fall into a pit."

A News reporter wanted the exclusive story on the pit.

A Fundamentalist said, "You deserve your pit."

A Calvinist said, "If you'd been saved you'd never fallen into that pit."

An Armenian said, "You were saved and you still

153

fell into that pit."

A Charismatic said, "Just confess that you're not in that pit."

A Realist came along and said, "Now that's a pit!"

An IRS man asked if he was paying taxes on the pit.

An evasive person came along and avoided the subject of the pit altogether.

A self-pity person said, "You haven't seen anything until you've seen my pit."

An Optimist said, "Things could be worse."

A Pessimist said, "Things will get worse."

But Jesus, seeing the man in the pit, reached out and took him by the hand, and lifted him out of that pit.

Jesus Christ came down from heaven to die on a cruel cross, to lift us up out of the darkness of sin into His marvelous light. The only completely satisfying response to evil is the cross of Christ. There a holy and loving God conquers the offense of the puzzle of evil. The One willing to die in our place frees us from sin and delivers us from the evil inside of us. In **Romans 8:32,** Paul insists that a God who loves us that dearly surely will take care of us. ***"He that spared not his own Son, but delivered him up for us all, how shall he not with him also freely give us all things?"*** This is one truth that Satan is presently fighting so hard to keep away from fallen mankind.

In closing, the most fruitful lesson to learn from the legacy of Angel Lucifer, however, is not where or why sin originated; but rather to be sure to not follow Satan's prideful example, which surely leads to eternal destruction. Often, the New Testament comments on the

Old, and vice versa. One of Paul's relatively few comments on Satan is his admonition to Timothy about the qualifications of a bishop or pastor (which we have already alluded to) *". . . not a novice, lest being puffed up with pride he fall into the same condemnation as the devil."* (1 Timothy 3:2, 6) I have heard it said that the reason why God didn't forgive the Devil was that Satan was too proud to ask for forgiveness. I think there's a lot of truth in that statement. I know that it's the sin of pride that holds many of us back from asking God to grant us the forgiveness Christ has already purchased for us at the cross of Calvary. I think a good way to close this message is to quote a few of the many passages in God's Word warning us of the dangers of pride, and lead us in a prayer of humbly receiving Christ's mercy, forgiveness, and love.

"Pride goes before destruction, and a haughty spirit before a fall." (Proverbs 16:18-19)

"The pride of your heart has deceived you." (Obadiah 1:3)

"Be clothed with humility, for 'God resists the proud, but gives grace to the humble.' Therefore humble yourselves under the mighty hand of God, that He may exalt you in due time." (1 Pet. 5:5-6)

Closing Prayer

"Dear God, I know I'm a sinner and I need forgiveness. I believe Jesus Christ died on the cross for me. Lord Jesus, forgive me for my sins and be my Savior. I receive You now as my Lord. I put my faith in You, Your death for me on the cross, and Your Word which declares, *'if you confess with your mouth the Lord Jesus and believe in your heart that God has raised Him from the dead, you will be saved; for with thc heart one believes unto righteousness, and with the mouth confession is made unto salvation.'* **(Romans 10:9,10)** Thank you for forgiving me. Amen."

APPENDIX

(Do the fact that this book is a novel rather than an essay, there are many valid points I have not covered, thus far. For this reason I have selected three clear, yet concise articles about the theological problem of evil from various sources.)

Appendix A

Encyclopedia Article On The Subject Of Evil

I. Introduction

Evil, that which is morally bad or wrong, or that which causes harm, pain, or misery. In theology, the problem of evil arises if it is accepted that evil exists in a universe governed by a supreme being who is both good and omnipotent. In a formulation of the problem attributed to the Greek philosopher Epicurus, either God can prevent evil and chooses not to (and therefore is not good) or chooses to prevent it and cannot (and therefore is not all-powerful).

II. Traditional Religious Solutions

The problem of evil has been a central concern of philosophers and of all the major religions. Some of the solutions proposed have rested on a denial either of the existence of evil or of the omnipotence of God. In Hindu

159

teaching, for instance, evil has no real existence, being part of the illusory world of phenomena. In the ancient Persian religion Zoroastrianism and the related ancient Middle Eastern sect known as Manichaeism, evil is attributed to the existence of an evil deity, against whom the good deity must struggle (Dualism). In the Book of Job, on the other hand, after Job's comforters offer dubious explanations of Job's undeserved suffering, the demand for an explanation is ultimately made to seem presumptuous, and the Scriptural writer suggests that God's ways are mysterious and beyond human understanding.

III. Saint Augustine

As Christian theology began to emerge in the 3rd and 4th centuries, the problem of evil became particularly challenging because Christianity was committed to the existence of an all-powerful, benevolent God but at the same time acknowledged the real existence of evil. At the end of the 4th century St. Augustine formulated the solution that has had the greatest influence on subsequent Christian thinkers. As a young man, Augustine had accepted the dualistic theology of Manichaeism. The later influence of Neoplatonism prepared him for his conversion to Christianity and his theological reconciliation of the Christian belief in a benevolent God, the creator of everything that exists, with the pervasive presence of evil in the world. According to Augustine, evil has not been created by God, whose creation is entirely good. Evil is the privation, or absence, of good, as darkness is the absence of light. It is possible, however, for something created good to diminish in goodness, to become corrupted, and evil has crept in when creatures endowed with free will—angels, such lesser spirits as demons, and human beings—turn away from higher, or more complete, goods and choose lesser, partial ones. Furthermore, according to Augustine, what at first appears to be evil may be understood as good in the context of eternity. From God's eternal perspective, everything is good.

IV. Later Arguments

Augustine's ideas strongly influenced later Roman Catholic theologians, such as Thomas Aquinas, and Reformation Protestant theologians, particularly John Calvin. In the 17th century, the German philosopher Gottfried Wilhelm Leibniz argued that God's power of creation was limited to logically possible worlds, and evil is a logically necessary part of the "best of all possible worlds." During the Enlightenment, these arguments came under attack by skeptics. Both the French philosopher Voltaire and the English philosopher David Hume rejected the idea that the immense amount of pain and suffering in human life can be justified because it forms part of a benevolent divine plan.

V. The 20th Century

The unprecedented scale of the wars and persecutions of the 20th century undermined the secular belief in inevitable progress and confronted philosophers and theologians once again with the problem of evil. In particular, the question of whether extreme suffering can ever be theologically justified has been raised with regard to the Holocaust. Some have speculated about the absence of God; others have recalled the idea in the Book of Job of the mysteriousness of God's ways. The problem of evil has thus returned as a major concern of contemporary theology.

APPENDIX B

THE PROBLEM OF EVIL

(An Outline)

I. Introduction

A. Many philosophers have held that the existence of evil in the universe is the "Achilles heel" of Christianity, and that it constitutes evidence for the non-existence of the Christian God. This problem has been expressed in the following syllogism:

> If God is all-good, he would destroy evil.
> If God is all-powerful, he could destroy evil.
> But evil is not destroyed.
> Therefore, such a God (all-good and all-powerful) does not exist.

Another equally troublesome syllogism for Christians is:

> God is the author of everything.
> Evil is something.
> Therefore, God is the author of evil.

Christians can accept the first two premises but not the third, hence the problem.

B. This tension between the existence of evil and the Christian God has been a major subject of the

Arts:

> Some excellent modern examples from literature are: Dostoyevsky's BROTHERS KARAMZOV, and Camus's THE PLAGUE

II. The Nature of the Problem

The problem stems from a seemingly insolvable tension due to the three following beliefs of historic Christianity:

A. God is a morally perfect being (holy). The goodness of God.

B. God is an omnipotent being (all-powerful). The greatness of God.

C. Evil is a reality in the universe. Three types:

> 1. Natural evil. The natural world is in a fallen state. Malevolence is witnessed in nature (Contrary to what the nature religions believe!).

> 2. Moral evil. Evil that is the result of the will of moral beings.

> 3. Metaphysical evil (i.e., the Devil and demons).

III. Types of solutions

A. Theodicies: A theodicy is a rational attempt by theists to exonerate God as being the source of evil. Basically, these attempts try to modify one or more of the above assertions about God. There are basically two types:

1. Those that modify the nature of God. Finite-godism. two types:

a. God is limited in power, but evil is real. This view is known as Process theology and is found in liberal Protestantism and liberal Judaism. (See the popular book: WHEN BAD THINGS HAPPEN TO GOOD PEOPLE). This view sees God as finite and in the process of struggling with evil. The triumph of good over evil depends on man's cooperation with God.

Critique: This view does not explain the origin of evil, nor is there any guarantee that good will ultimately triumph over evil. The news reports would seem to argue against this view.

b. God is limited in his goodness. He is detached from his creation. Forms of Deism and Sadism.

Critique: If this is true (that God is finite) then the good cannot be known. To know the good necessitates an infinite, absolute standard.

2. Those that re-define the nature of evil.

a. Evil is really good. Evil, i.e., suffering, brings about good, therefore, evil itself is good.

Critique: There is no real difference between good and evil. The Bible warns against making evil good and good, evil.

b. Evil comes from Satan. This results in a dualism which teaches that good and evil are equal.

Critique: (1) It limits God's power. (2) No redemption or victory over evil is possible, only an eternal struggle.

c. Evil must exist to appreciate the good. There is certainly some truth to this. However: Critique: (1) This too, makes evil a good. (2) The end justifies the means.

B. Irrational Approaches

1. Evil is an illusion. This is the teaching of Eastern philosophy and religion, and the "Made in America" cult, Christian Science.

Critique: (1) But isn't the illusion real? Where did the illusion originate? Is there a practical difference if evil is an illusion or real? (2) No assertions can be made about good or evil. (3) If evil is an illusion why fight it?

2. Atheist position: Evil is not a thing in itself.

Critique: We must note that the problem of evil is devastating for atheism. His problem is twice compounded. Since there is no ultimate good, any definition is arbitrary. His only logical recourse is nihilism, i.e. meaninglessness.
Atheists, however, in order to live their

everyday lives smuggle in values from other worldviews.

C. The Faith Approach

1. The Goodness and Greatness of God, and reality of evil, are affirmed, but the origin and purpose of evil are a mystery. Something less than a complete resolution will have to suffice for the here and now.

a. Defense

(1) While it may not be possible to resolve the problem, we may alleviate it somewhat, and may see the direction from which final solutions might come had we more complete knowledge and understanding.

(2) God is omnipotent, but this does not mean God can do anything. He cannot do that which is illogical, like make a square circle. Likewise, how can he make a man with free choice and at the same time guarantee that he will always do exactly what God desires?

(3) If God had not included evil as a part of His plan He would have to have made man other than what he is. To God it was better to make man rather than androids.

(4) God could eradicate evil, but to do so might itself be an evil. A good person does not always eliminate all the evil he possible can. Some suffering, for example can lead to higher good.

(5) Some of what we term good and evil may not actually be that. We are finite. What is "good"? and what is "evil"? There is also a time element. Things must be evaluated in the light of eternity.

(6) Evil is contingent, not a thing in itself, a negation of that which is good, but real nonetheless. Blindness, for example, is real but it is a lack of something. It is quite conceivable that God included evil, the lack of good, in His plan without being evil Himself. In other words, some Christian philosophers say that God did not exhaust Himself when He created the universe. He could have created an infinite number of possibilities. This is not the best He

169

could have done; it is however, perfect
for what He designed it for.

(7) The world as it now is, is not as it was
when God created it. It is now in an
unnatural state due to the fall of man.

(8) Christianity's teaching on the hereafter
allows for ultimate justice. Evil will
be punished; good will triumph.

(9) Christians can have reasons for believing
that God has reasons for allowing evil,
even if we do not always know what they
are. We can trust Him because of what we
know about Him from Revelation, and from
our relational experience with Him.

   b. Problems

(1) How could Adam have sinned if he were
created good? This is a profound
mystery. Willing is related to desiring.
Where did the desire to disobey come
from?

(2) Why didn't God just make the world
originally like Christians believe heaven
is to be? We can only speculate as to
why He created at all, or why He made the

world as it is. The answer may lie in the expression of His attributes. How could He express His Grace if He would have originally made earth like heaven? Or His justice? etc. There would not have been a need.

Conclusion: As finite beings we only see a small portion of the Divine weaving, and that the underside!

Outline #39 © Christian Information Ministries, 2050 N. Collins Blvd. #100, Richardson, TX 75080. http://www.fni.com/cim/ Used by permission.

APPENDIX C

THE PROBLEM OF EVIL:

How Can A Good God Allow Evil?

Introduction

John Stott has said that "the fact of suffering undoubtedly constitutes the single greatest challenge to the Christian faith." It is unquestionably true that there is no greater obstacle to faith than that of the reality of evil and suffering in the world. Indeed, even for the believing Christian, there is no greater test of faith than this--that the God who loves him permits him to suffer, at times in excruciating ways...Why does a good God allow his creatures, and even His children to suffer?

First, it's important to distinguish between two kinds of evil: moral evil and natural evil. Moral evil results from the actions of free creatures. Murder, rape and theft are examples. Natural evil results from natural processes such as earthquakes and floods. Of course, sometimes the two are intermingled, such as when flooding results in loss of human life due to poor planning or shoddy construction of buildings.

It's also important to identify two aspects of the problem of evil and suffering. First, there is the philosophical or apologetic aspect. This is the problem of evil approached from the standpoint of the skeptic who challenges the possibility or probability that a God exists who would allow such suffering. In meeting this apologetic challenge we must utilize the tools of reason and evidence in "giving a reason for the hope within us." (I Pet. 3:15)

Second is the religious or emotional aspect of the problem of evil. This is the problem of evil approached from the standpoint of the believer whose faith in God is severely tested by trial. How can we love and worship God when He allows us to suffer in these ways? In meeting the religious/emotional challenge we must appeal to the truth revealed by God in Scripture. We will address both aspects of the problem of evil in this essay.

It's also helpful to distinguish between two types of the philosophical or apologetic aspect of the problem of evil. The first is the logical challenge to belief in God. This challenge says it is irrational and hence impossible to believe in the existence of a good and powerful God on the basis of the existence of evil in the world. The logical challenge is usually posed in the form of a statement such as this:

1. **A good God would destroy evil.**

2. **An all powerful God could destroy evil.**

3. **Evil is not destroyed.**

4. **Therefore, there cannot possibly be such a good and powerful God.**

It is logically impossible to believe that both evil,

and a good and powerful God exist in the same reality, for such a God certainly could and would destroy evil.

On the other hand, the evidential challenge contends that while it may be rationally possible to believe such a God exists, it is highly improbable or unlikely that He does. We have evidence of so much evil that is seemingly pointless and of such horrendous intensity. For what valid reason would a good and powerful God allow the amount and kinds of evil which we see around us?

These issues are of an extremely important nature-- not only as we seek to defend our belief in God, but also as we live out our Christian lives.

The Logical Problem of Evil

We have noted that there are two aspects of the problem of evil: the philosophical or apologetic, and the religious or emotional aspect. We also noted that within the philosophical aspect there are two types of challenges to faith in God: the logical and the evidential.

David Hume, the eighteenth century philosopher, stated the logical problem of evil when he inquired about God, "Is He willing to prevent evil, but not able? Then He is impotent. Is He able, but not willing? Then He is malevolent. Is He both able and willing? Whence then is evil?" When the skeptic challenges belief in God on the basis of the logical problem of evil, he is suggesting that it is irrational or logically impossible to believe in the existence of both a good and all powerful God and in the reality of evil and suffering. Such a God would not possibly allow evil to exist.

The key to the resolution of this apparent conflict is to recognize that when we say God is all powerful, we do not imply that He is capable of doing anything imaginable. True, Scripture states that "with God all things are possible" (Mt. 19:26). But Scripture also states that there are some things God cannot do. For instance, God cannot lie (Tit. 1:2). Neither can He be tempted to sin, nor can He tempt others to sin (James 1:13). In other words, He cannot do anything that is "out of character" for a righteous God. Neither can He do anything that is out of character for a rational being in a rational world. Certainly even God cannot "undo the past," or create a square triangle, or make what is false true. He cannot do what is irrational or absurd.

And it is on this basis that we conclude that God could not eliminate evil without at the same time rendering it impossible to accomplish other goals which are important to Him. Certainly, for God to create beings in his own image, who are capable of sustaining a personal relationship with Him, they must be beings who are capable of freely loving Him and following his will without coercion. Love or obedience on any other basis would not be love or obedience at all, but mere compliance. But creatures who are free to love God must also be free to hate or ignore Him. Creatures who are free to follow His will must also be free to reject it. And when people act in ways outside the will of God, great evil and suffering is the ultimate result. This line of thinking is known as the "free will defense" concerning the problem of evil.

But what about natural evil--evil resulting from natural processes such as earthquakes, floods and diseases? Here it is important first to recognize that we live in a fallen world, and that we are subject to natural disasters that would not have occurred had man not chosen to rebel against God. Even so, it is difficult to imagine how we could function as free creatures in a world much different than our own--a world in which consistent natural processes allow us to predict with some certainty the consequences of our choices and actions. Take the law of gravity, for instance. This is a natural process without which we could not possibly function as human beings, yet under some circumstances it is also capable of resulting in great harm.

Certainly, God is capable of destroying evil--but not without destroying human freedom, or a world in which free creatures can function. And most agree that this line of reasoning does successfully respond to the challenge of the logical problem of evil.

The Evidential Problem of Evil

While most agree that belief in a good and powerful God is rationally possible, nonetheless many contend that the existence of such a God is improbable due to the nature of the evil which we see in the world about us. They conclude that if such a God existed it is highly unlikely that He would allow the amount and intensity of evil which we see in our world. Evil which frequently seems to be of such a purposeless nature.

This charge is not to be taken lightly, for evidence abounds in our world of evil of such a horrendous nature that it is difficult at times to fathom what possible purpose it could serve. However, difficult as this aspect of the problem of evil is, careful thinking will show that there are reasonable responses to this challenge.

Surely it is difficult for us to understand why God would allow some things to happen. But simply because we find it difficult to imagine what reasons God could have for permitting them, does not mean that no such reasons exist. It is entirely possible that such reasons are not only beyond our present knowledge, but also beyond our present ability to understand. A child does not always understand the reasons that lie behind all that his father allows or does not allow him to do. It would be unrealistic for us to expect to understand all of God's reasons for allowing all that He does. We do not fully understand many things about the world we live in--what lies behind the force of gravity for instance, or the exact function of subatomic particles. Yet we believe in these physical realities.

Beyond this, however, we can suggest possible reasons for God allowing some of the horrendous evils which do exist in our world. Perhaps there are people who would never sense their utter dependence on God apart from experiencing the intense pain that they do in life (Ps. 119:71). Perhaps there are purposes that God intends to accomplish among his angelic or demonic creatures which require his human creatures to experience some of the things that we do (Job 1-2). It may be that the suffering we experience in this life is somehow preparatory to our existence in the life to come (2 Cor. 4:16-18). Even apart from the revelation of Scripture, these are all possible reasons behind God's permission of evil. And at any rate, most people agree that there is much more good in the world than evil--at least enough good to make life well worth the living.

In responding to the challenge to belief in God based on the intensity and seeming purposelessness of much evil in the world, we must also take into account all of the positive evidence that points to his existence: the evidence of design in nature, the historical evidence for the reliability of Scripture and of the resurrection of Jesus Christ. In light of the totality of the evidence, it certainly cannot be proven that there are no sufficient reasons for God's allowing the amount of evil that we see in the world...or even that it is improbable that such reasons exist.

The Religious Problem of Evil - Part I

But the existence of evil and suffering in our world poses more than a merely philosophical or apologetic problem. It also poses a very personal religious and emotional problem for the person who is enduring great

179

trial. Although our painful experience may not challenge our belief that God exists, what may be at risk is our confidence in a God we can freely worship and love, and in whose love we can feel secure. Much harm can be done when we attempt to aid a suffering brother or sister by merely dealing with the intellectual aspects of this problem, or when we seek to find solace for ourselves in this way. Far more important than answers about the nature of God, is a revelation of the love of God--even in the midst of trial. And as God's children, it is not nearly as important what we say about God as what we do to manifest his love.

First, it is evident from Scripture that when we suffer it is not unnatural to experience emotional pain, nor is it unspiritual to express it. It is noteworthy for instance that there are nearly as many psalms of lament as there are psalms of praise and thanksgiving, and these two sentiments are mingled together in many places (cf. Pss. 13, 88). Indeed, the psalmist encourages us to "pour out our hearts to God" (Ps. 62:8). And when we do, we can be assured that God understands our pain. Jesus Himself keenly felt the painful side of life. When John the Baptist was beheaded it is recorded that "He withdrew to a lonely place" obviously to mourn his loss (Mt. 14:13). And when his friend Lazarus died, it is recorded that Jesus openly wept at his tomb (Jn. 11:35). Even though He was committed to following the Father's will to the cross, He confessed to being filled with anguish of soul in contemplating it (Mt. 26:38). It is not without reason that Jesus was called "a man of sorrows and acquainted with grief" (Isa. 53:3); and we follow in his steps when we truthfully acknowledge our own pain.

We cross the line, however, from sorrow to sin when we allow our grief to quench our faith in God, or follow the counsel that Job was offered by his wife when she told him to "curse God and die" (Job 2:9b).

Secondly, when we suffer we should draw comfort from reflecting on Scriptures which assure us that God knows and cares about our situation, and promises to be with us to comfort and uphold us. The psalmist tells us that "the Lord is near to the brokenhearted" (Ps. 34:18), and that when we go through the "valley of the shadow of death" it is then that his presence is particularly promised to us (Ps. 23:4). Speaking through the prophet Isaiah, the Lord said, "Can a woman forget her nursing child, and have no compassion on the son of her womb? Even these may forget, but I will not forget you" (Isa. 49:15). He is more mindful of us than is a nursing mother toward her child! It is of the One whom we know as the "God of all comfort and Father of mercies" that Peter speaks when He bids us to cast our anxieties on Him, "for He cares for us" (1 Pet. 5:7). Our cares are his personal concern!

The Religious Problem of Evil - Part II

We noted that when suffering strikes it is neither unnatural to experience emotional pain, nor unspiritual to express it. But we also noted that when suffering strikes, we must be quick to reflect on the character of God and on the promises He gives to those who are enduring great trial. Now we want to focus on one of the great truths of God's word--that even in severe trial God is working all things together for the good of those who love him (Rom. 8:28). This is not at all to imply that evil is somehow good. But it does mean that we are to recognize that even in what is evil God is at work to bring about His good purposes in our lives.

Joseph gave evidence of having learned this truth when after years of unexplained suffering due to the betrayal of his brothers, he was able to say to them, "You meant it for evil, but God meant it for good" (Gen. 50:20). Though God did not cause his brothers to betray him, nonetheless He was able to use it in furthering His good intentions.

This is the great hope we have in the midst of suffering, that in a way beyond our comprehension, God is able to turn evil against itself. And it is because of this truth that we can find joy even in the midst of sorrow and pain. The apostle Paul described himself as "sorrowful, yet always rejoicing" (2 Cor. 6:10). And we are counseled to rejoice in trial, not because the affliction itself is a cause for joy (it is not), but because in it God can find an occasion for producing what is good.

What are some of those good purposes suffering promotes? For one, suffering can provide an opportunity for God to display his glory-- to make evident his mercy, faithfulness, power and love in the midst of painful circumstances (Jn. 9:1-3). Suffering can also allow us to give proof of the genuineness of our faith, and even serve to purify our faith (1 Pet. 1:7). As in the case of Job, our faithfulness in trial shows that we serve Him not merely for the benefits He offers, but for the love of God Himself (Job 1:9-11). Severe trial also provides an opportunity for believers to demonstrate their love for one another as members of the body of Christ who "bear one another's burdens" (1 Cor 12:26; Gal. 6:2). Indeed, as D.A. Carson has said, "experiences of suffering... engender compassion and empathy..., and make us better able to help others" (Carson, 122). As we are comforted by God in affliction, so we are better able to comfort others (2 Cor. 1:4). Suffering also plays a key role in developing godly virtues, and in deterring us from sin. Paul recognized that his "thorn in the flesh" served to keep him from boasting, and promoted true humility and dependence on God (2 Cor. 12:7). The psalmist recognized that his affliction had increased his determination to follow God's will (Ps. 119:71). Even Jesus "learned obedience from the things He suffered" (Heb. 5:8). As a man He learned by experience the value of submitting to the will of God, even when it was the most difficult thing in the world to do.

Finally, evil and suffering can awaken in us a greater hunger for heaven, and for that time when God's purposes for these experiences will have been finally fulfilled, when pain and sorrow shall be no more (Rev. 21:4).

The Final WORD:

And there was war in heaven: Michael and his angels fought against the dragon; and the dragon fought and his angels,

And prevailed not; neither was their place found any more in heaven.

And the great dragon was cast out, that old serpent, called the Devil, and Satan, which deceiveth the whole world: he was cast out into the earth, and his angels were cast out with him.

And I heard a loud voice saying in heaven, "Now is come salvation, and strength, and the kingdom of our God, and the power of his Christ: for the accuser of our brethren is cast down, which accused them before our God day and night."

And they overcame him by the blood of the Lamb, and by the word of their testimony; and they loved not their lives unto the death.

Revelation 12:7-12

Also available by Charles Simpson

Christian Island

Parables About Pride,
Gossip & Discontentment

Charles Simpson

In the Sea of Humanity, off the coast of Mammon, there's an island called Christian, where Mr. Saved Soul is the Mayor. Because of its beautiful beaches and abundant orchards, this island's reputation became much larger than its actual size.

Thus begins the first of three parables in which Mayor Saved Soul of Christian Island learns how to overcome pride, gossip and discontentment. The setting is on Christian Island, a tranquil place where the Mayor serves under the care and authority of the great King. Although the following stories are intentionally light and friendly, don't be fooled! The truths they contain are life changing. (See page 189 for ordering.)

About The Author

Pastor Charles Simpson was raised in Tennessee and became a Christian in high school in the late 70's. Soon after graduating, he moved to New York City to be a missionary in the Big Apple. While on staff at Times Square Church he married his wife, Lynn. He has planted three churches: in the South Bronx, in Scottsdale, Arizona and in Astoria, Queens where he and his wife now live and pastor Hope Chapel, Queens Foursquare Church.
(E-mail address: charlessimpson@juno.com)

About Ordering This Book

Copies of this book (and Christian Island) can be conveniently purchased through the Internet site of Amazon Books which is www.amazon.com. Type in the book name and follow the directions.

Or this book can be purchased through Ascribe Publishing. The price is $10.00 per book, which will pay all costs, including taxes, shipping and handling. A check or money order should be made out to Ascribe Publishing, P.O. Box 5726, L.I.C., NY, 11105. Call (718) 932-3732 for quantity discounts or visit our web site at:

http://homestead.juno.com/ascribepublishing

*(Bookstores can order from Spring Arbor
Distributors at 1-800-395-5599.)*

Pillowcase

We are taught it will be loud,
but sometimes violence is as
quiet as your face against the
pillowcase.

Stripped

I died in your bed.
There will be no choirs,
no crows, no foxes, no cops.
Just the grave of my body,
stripped down to my socks.
I died in your bed,
then walked to the bathroom
and bled.
There will be no stains,
no sinew, no tissue, just bone.
But I'll make a splint
to carry me home.
I died in your bed,
but you won't find my body.
I'll dig up my grave and all
I embody.

Shrike

Would it have been easier
if you had the beak of a shrike
or the teeth of a wolf?
Would it have been easier
if you looked like a monster?

Predator

I didn't understand the word
predator until I watched you hunt.

I didn't know you were hunting
until I was the prey.

I didn't know I was the prey
until I was in your teeth.

Tell me,
did you pick my bones clean?

Irrefutable

I was raised steeped in
privilege, anointed with
the promise that my body
belonged to me. There were
signs it was a lie,
but nothing until that night
that was irrefutable proof.

Taking

This isn't the taking,
this is the unmaking.

Snare

Your mask was a
gruesome symphony,

your harp string throat
tuned to draw me in and
snare me.

I should have known
when I heard the drum
of your pulse,

you were hollow.

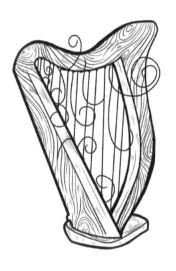

Three, Three

Half past three and
there is blood between
my thighs.

Half past two and
I'm telling myself lies.

Half past one and
the mirror stares back.

Half past twelve and
my eyes have gone black.

Half past eleven and
I'm leaving your apartment.

Half past ten. *I lose time.*

Half past nine and
collapsed on your couch.

Half past eight and
you are inside my mouth.

Half past seven and
I don't know my name.

Half past six and
I want someone to blame.

Half past five and
you call yourself a sinner.

Half past four and
the air is getting thinner.

Half past three and
there is blood between
my thighs.

Petrified

Sometimes,
the only way to fight
is to close your eyes.

Content Warning

Rape
Sexual Assault
Rape Culture
PTSD
Depression
Anxiety
Suicidal Thoughts

For Christine

Sovereign

He felled me like a
monarch, my body the
kingdom.

Daze

I remember
the ride home like old film
skipping and splintering.

The city looked so peaceful
in a predawn daze.

Sleepy taxis, bleary shop windows,
bodega flowers in plastic veils.

Lilies, baby's breath, alstroemeria.
Lilies, baby's breath, alstroemeria.

Nothing But

I once held a friend
in my lap, swearing to
her that it was not her
fault.

When I woke to find
a reddish brown crust
between my legs, I
begged with paper gods
for it to be my fault.

A misunderstanding.
A miscommunication.
A misstep on my part.

I begged for it to be
anything, *anything* but.

When I came to I had
nothing but the truth.

He raped me, and my
body was proof.

Valkyrie

They say to behold a Valkyrie
is to stare unflinching into flame.

Tell me, does this fire barrel through
my veins?

Have I missed something? Some war
horn from beyond?

Because my eyes have burnt out,
and my words are gone.

What I Said

I thought about us a lot last night, and I don't think this is gonna work out. I like you, but I was kind of uncomfortable with some of the things that happened when we were having sex. I'm not saying you like raped me or anything, but I think maybe there was a little selective deafness on your part. I'm sure it wasn't on purpose. I'm sorry. Please don't contact me again unless you need me.

What I Wish I Had Said

Micro Cuts

I am raw. Each step is
a chafe, a stitch, a scream
of these micro cuts you
left in me.

Smoke in the Sun

Rally the infantry,
set my brain on fire,
cull these memories,
split these wires.
Watch from above
as I shed this form
like smoke in the sun.

Ruins

I'm okay.

Say it until the words run
like paint or ink or kids with
guns.

I'm okay.

Say it until your teeth wear down
like ruins or tires or doused forest
fires.

I'm okay.

Alstroemeria

I never gave her a funeral.
She deserved one, I suppose.
Nearly twenty-two years she
spent among my bones.

I never gave her a funeral.
No coffins or choirs, just a
cradle in the cold dark soil.

I never gave her a funeral,
and perhaps I never will.

If I did, I would sing her to sleep.
If I did, I would plant alstroemeria
at her feet.

Post Traumatic

I start to lose words.

Syllables, sentences reel back to
the safety of my muted throat.

Nightmares roll in like thunder,
or frost down the mountainside.

A hissing cat takes up residence in
the alleys of my ribcage.

I lash out, I cave in, I lose words, I
break and I break and I break again.

Sheets

I want to make this pretty for you.
I want to tell you I found a lover to
kiss it better.
I want to promise the sun will lift you
from your sheets.
I want to show you this world is kind.
The trouble is, I don't want to lie.

Snap

A twig snaps in the hollows
of my mind and I am gone.
Logic erodes, oxygen follows.
The hair on my arms stands
at his touch, which I
know, I *know*, is there. Don't
tell me he isn't here, don't tell
me everything is alright. I feel
it, I feel him, in my skin at night.

Fill Line

There has to be a threshold,
a ceiling for the pain inflicted
on one person.
Is someone keeping track?
Does anyone know my tally?
Don't fill past this line,
I'll overflow; you'll overwhelm me.

Chameleons

Time chews through memory
like wildfire. This is normal, they
tell me, a defense against the
unbearable. Chameleons have
camouflage, we have amnesia.

Hallowed Ground

I never told you,
but I was ready to go.

The ground called
from five stories below,

I heard it through
my floorboards.

I heard the clatter of
little yellow pills

clamoring for the
cushion of my tongue.

I'm glad I stayed,
but I can't pretend
it was easy.

The Forest

The trouble is, this only works
half the time. After the wildfires,
the forests rise. The trees are made
of hands and teeth. When the wind
blows, they seem to speak.
You're a good girl, aren't you?

Mirror, Mirror

I don't know who I am
when I'm not suffering.

Think of Me

I wonder if you think of me.

I wonder what I want you to
think of me.

Do I want you on your knees,
begging forgiveness from a god
who cannot answer?

Do I want you on your toes,
knowing your name is at the back
of my throat?

Would it be better if you never
thought of me at all?

I wonder if you think of me,

and if you do, am I in my grave?

Eggshell Ballet

Someone show me the line
between victim and survivor.
Because each day, I find, is a
ballet on eggshells.
Someone show me the line
between breathing and aching.
If you keep it between us,
I think they're the same.

Flaws

For all of my thorns,
for all my flaws,
I know I am a lion
for the ones I love.
I am the salt ring at
their feet.
I am the apparition
that keeps their
demons from sleep.
So why was I a lamb
when my devil bared
his teeth?

Liminal Space

My body is liminal space
like a train station or a deli or
a 7-Eleven at three in the morning.
My body is liminal space
for passersby. Sometimes they
love me, sometimes they hurt me,
and they never stay.

Glass

I talk about him like I am
spitting up chunks of glass.

Regret

I want to be angry.
I want to relish making him squirm.

I want to hear the thunderclap
of the gavel, the rattling clang of his
cell door.

I want to roll his regret like a blunt,
smoke it from a Brooklyn rooftop.

I want to want those things.

Instead,

I scrawl blame across the curve of my hips,
the flat of my stomach, the run of my thighs.

Instead,

I tell myself centuries of lies.

Over

Am I overreacting?
After all, it could have
been worse. Blood still
rattles through my veins.
I never thought I was a
coward. I always saw
myself as brave. So why
do I still cringe at every
touch? Why do I still
dread every day?

Hey Girl

When I pick up the pace,
cast my eyes down, or walk
the other way,
it isn't because I can't take a
joke or am having a bad day.
It would be no different if you
were better looking, younger,
or perfect in every way.
I run because in your leering
mouth, I see him.
In your *compliments*, I hear him.
In your every move, I feel him.
For all I know, you are him.

Chorus

What is it about rape
that shreds us to the core?
Maybe because there is
never a good reason, never
another door. It can't be justified,
it can't be reduced, it can't be
ignored. It says *you are nothing*,
and you echo the chorus.

Splinters, Thorns

These words are nothing but
splinters and thorns. My skin
weeps as I uproot them. The
barbs clatter, chatter, as they
hit the floor of this paper cocoon.

Ghosts in the Attic

The detective asks why
I waited so long to report.
Judgement sticks like summat
in her teeth, and her questions
groan like ghosts in the attic.
Why did you stay?
What did you wear?
Had you had sex before?
Why were you there?
The detective asks why
I waited so long to report.
The answer I choke on is *people
like her.*

Survivor

Tonight, I don't want to be a survivor.
I want to make a bed of the cobwebs at
the back of my closet.
I'm tired of moving, of grieving, of loss.
I'm tired of what is, what isn't, what was.
Tonight, I don't want to be a survivor,
but want, she tells me, just isn't a factor.
I am what I am, and I am what you are,
a world, a heart, a sword, an altar.

Control Call

Nothing about this screams
control.

The frantic sprint of the timer
on the screen,

the flutter of the fluorescents
high above me,

the drone of the detective, polite,
detached.

Then comes his voice, a quiet kind
of death.

No one expects the monster to speak
poetry.

No, not poetry, politics.

The language of the in between,
the art of the almost answer.

No confessions, no denials, nothing
so simple as a *yes* or a *no*.

It Follows

Let me be clear,
there is no mistake
in rape.

It is not a blip of
ignorance.

It is not speaking out
of turn.

It is not a notion to be
unlearned.

Let me be clear,
there is no mistake
in rape.

If his *choice* should not
hound him, where is my
reprieve?

Absolution

My forgiveness is not owed.
Not to him, not to this culture
of violence, of silence.

Doubt

Your tongue stiff with fear
is not a *yes*, just like your skirt
your heels, your dress. A kiss
is not a pact, and a touch is
not a contract. A *yes* is not a
yes in the shadow of a threat,
and a *maybe* from this morning
is not an unanswered debt. A
no is a *no* whispered, screamed,
or choked out. A *no* is a *no* if a
yes is in doubt.

Goner

I'm a goner
neck deep in
the sound.

I'm a goner
with dust I'll
be crowned.

I'm a goner
both faces
are blurred.

I'm a goner
in trenches I
burn.

I'm a goner
without a way
home.

I'm a goner
but at least
I'm not alone.

Inspired by Goner/Leave the City by Twenty One Pilots

Fables

This is only complicated
because you want it to be.

This is only complicated
because you crave leniency.

Blurred lines, mixed signals,
no means *yes* and other fables
designed to keep this under
the table.

This isn't complicated.

If she doesn't say *yes*,
if she doesn't kiss back,
if she cries to herself,
or goes still, cold, flat,

if she shrinks from your touch,
passes out on the floor,
if she is too young to understand,
or too drunk to want more,

there is no excuse to take what
you want.

This isn't complicated.

Group

We could sit in silence
from here until spring and
you would still know all the
darkest corners of me.

Disclaimer

Leave your disclaimers
on the front porch.
You don't need them here.
Here, you are home.

It could have been worse,
it could always be worse,
but you're allowed to grieve.
You're allowed to mourn.

Stonecold

If this were about
what she wore
where she was
what she drank

it would only happen
to girls in miniskirts
under overpasses
on the heels of vodka.

It would not happen
to girls in sweatpants
in their apartments
stone cold sober.

It would not happen
to boys.

It would not have happened
to me in my warmups after
practice.

It would not have happened
to me in my high waisted
jeans in his bright studio.

Harpoon

This is for you,

the ones swept under the rug
because their story isn't pretty,
or they're from the wrong side
of town.

The ones who swallow the truth
because they need this job or they
have no proof.

The ones who raised their voices
only to be buried alive, because
the truth is a harpoon to their

centuries of lies.

This is for you.

Anniversary

It will be one year soon,
and I won't lie. Sometimes,
it still feels like yesterday.
Sometimes, it still feels like
today.

But the breathing is coming
easier, and the living follows.

More

I won't tell you that you
are made of starlight or
magic or a feathered breeze.

This is messy, and mad, and
ugly, and mean.

This is life, and it isn't fair,
and it shouldn't happen, but

it does, it does, it does.

I won't tell you that you
are made of starlight, because
you are so much more.

You are stubborn and brave
and impossible to ignore, but
most of all, you are *more*.

Handle with Care

I am trying.
I am trying to move on.
I am trying not to flinch
at the prick of hazel eyes.
I am trying not to be sick
when I hear a certain song.
I am trying not to unravel.
I am trying not to be gone.
This isn't for attention,
there is nothing here to gain.
Please, please, understand
there is a war in my brain.

Better Days

I know you are hurting.
I know the chasm in your
chest, your soul, your breast.
I know each dawn is a weight
on your back.
I know better days are too far
to have or to hold.
But if you stand still, silent in the
trees,
I swear you can hear them calling
your name.

Reclaim

I am reclaiming the arch of my back,
the swell of my chest,
the untamed vibrato of my breath.

Valkyrie (Reprise)

They say to behold a Valkyrie
is to stare unflinching into flame.

I am not forged of a legend,
but there is worth in my veins.

There is no war horn from beyond,
but this is a battle cry

for my sisters, for my brothers,
for my siblings who are despite it all

alive.

Cathedrals

I collect my stained glass bones
piece them together with fever,
with fervor.
I build myself a cathedral—I am
the spire, the altar, the incense, the fire.

Be Okay

It will never be okay.
There will never come
a day I am not
irrevocably changed,
but the hurt is not final.
His touch was not fatal.
Take my hand. There are
horizons to chase, oceans
to swallow. There are songs
to write, love to make, and
hearts to follow.
It will never be okay,
but I—*you*—will be.

Resources

You do not have to go through this alone. The resources listed below are *free*, *confidential*, and *accessible* from a phone or computer.

RAINN (Rape, Incest, and Abuse National Network)

The largest anti sexual violence organization in the United States. In partnership with more than 1,000 local sexual assault service providers, it operates the National Sexual Assault Hotline.

1-(800)-HOPE (4673)

Chat: www.hotline.rainn.org

SAFE HORIZON

Offers counselling, legal resources, and shelter to victims of sexual violence, human trafficking, and other forms of violence.

1-(800)-621-HOPE (4673)

Website: www.safehorizon.org

FORGE

The national sexual violence helpline for transgender and nonbinary survivors.

Website: www.forge-forward.org

1IN6

The national sexual violence helpline for male survivors.

Website: www.1in6.org

THE TREVOR PROJECT

National hotline for LGBTQ+ youth considering suicide or self-harm.

1-(866)-488-7386

Website: www.thetrvorproject.org

SCESA (National Organization of Sisters of Color Ending Sexual Assault)

An advocacy organization for women of color who are survivors of sexual or domestic violence.

Website: www.sisterslead.org

Acknowledgements

Acknowledgements are always tough, but this time I don't even know where to begin. How do you thank the people who walked with you through your darkest days? Guess I'll give it a shot.

Mom, you were the first person I called after it happened, and your empathy and steadfastness set the tone for my recovery. Every day since you have been my rock. Thank you.

Dad, you have been so patient with me. If you made it to the end of this book, you have done more than I ever could have asked. Thank you.

Christine, my therapist. I'm so lucky I found you. You steadied me when I was coming apart at the seams. I wish every survivor had access to someone like you.

My therapy group, my Creamless Creampuffs (long story). We met under the worst circumstances, but somehow, we managed to forge a bond that went beyond anything I have ever experienced. We laughed, cried, screamed, I threw a tissue box on the ground, and somehow, we healed each other, if only a little.

My friends. Dani, Evan, Mackenzie, Sarah, Noah, Maya, Jennifer, Allie, Zoe, Annmarie, Beverly, and whoever I'm surely forgetting, thank you so much for your continued love and support.

My fantastic beta readers. Alicia Cook, McKayla Debonis, Jenna Clare, Morgan Nikola-Wren, J.R. Rouge, and K.Y. Robinson, thank you so much for lending your time and words to this little book. Your support meant everything to me. I look up to all of you as poets and people.

Suzy, the wonderful artist who illustrated this book. I'm so glad I stumbled across your account. You're a talented artist, and a generous soul. Collaborating with you has been an absolute privilege.

To Tyler Joseph and Josh Dun of Twenty One Pilots. *Sahlo Folina.*

Thank you to my readers for sticking with me.

Lastly, thank you to the millions of survivors of sexual violence who wake up every morning and choose to keep fighting. You are more than your trauma, and your life will be more than your fight. Keep going.